T0023584

THE PELICAN SHAKESPEARE
GENERAL EDITORS

STEPHEN ORGEL
A. R. BRAUNMULLER

King Lear

A Conflated Text

Henry Irving in one of his most spectacular productions, at the Lyceum, 1892. The settings, designed by the Pre-Raphaelite painter Ford Madox Brown, were archeologically accurate scenes of early Britain, and complex stage machinery and lighting effects were employed throughout. *(Drawing by J. Bernard Partridge)*

William Shakespeare

King Lear

A Conflated Text

EDITED BY STEPHEN ORGEL

PENGUIN BOOKS

PENGUIN BOOKS
An imprint of Penguin Random House LLC
375 Hudson Street
New York, New York 10014
penguin.com

The Tragedy of King Lear edited by Alfred Harbage
published in Penguin Books (USA) 1958
Revised edition published 1970
This edition edited by Stephen Orgel published 1999

Copyright © 1958, 1970, 1999 by Penguin Random House LLC
Penguin supports copyright. Copyright fuels creativity, encourages diverse voices, promotes free speech, and creates a vibrant culture. Thank you for buying an authorized edition of this book and for complying with copyright laws by not reproducing, scanning, or distributing any part of it in any form without permission. You are supporting writers and allowing Penguin to continue to publish books for every reader.

ISBN 978-0-14-312855-7

Printed in the United States of America

15 17 19 20 18 16

Set in Adobe Garamond
Designed by Virginia Norey

Contents

Publisher's Note vii

The Theatrical World ix

The Texts of Shakespeare xxv

Introduction xxix

Note on the Text xliii

King Lear 1

Publisher's Note

THE PELICAN SHAKESPEARE has served generations of readers as an authoritative series of texts and scholarship since the first volume appeared under the general editorship of Alfred Harbage over half a century ago. In the past decades, new editions followed to reflect the profound changes textual and critical studies of Shakespeare have undergone. The texts of the plays and poems were thoroughly revised in accordance with leading scholarship, and in some cases were entirely reedited. New introductions and notes were provided in all the volumes. The Pelican Shakespeare was designed as a successor to the original series; the previous editions had been taken into account, and the advice of the previous editors was solicited where it was feasible to do so. The current editions include updated bibliographic references to recent scholarship.

Certain textual features of the new Pelican Shakespeare should be particularly noted. All lines are numbered that contain a word, phrase, or allusion explained in the glossarial notes. In addition, for convenience, every tenth line is also numbered, in italics when no annotation is indicated. The intrusive and often inaccurate place headings inserted by early editors are omitted (as has become standard practice), but for the convenience of those who miss them, an indication of locale now appears as the first item in the annotation of each scene.

In the interest of both elegance and utility, each speech prefix is set in a separate line when the speakers' lines are in verse, except when those words form the second half of a verse line. Thus the verse form of the speech is kept visually intact. What is printed as verse and what is printed as prose has, in general, the authority of the original texts. Departures from the original texts in this regard have the authority only of editorial tradition and the judgment of the Pelican editors; and, in a few instances, are admittedly arbitrary.

The Theatrical World

ECONOMIC REALITIES determined the theatrical world in which Shakespeare's plays were written, performed, and received. For centuries in England, the primary theatrical tradition was nonprofessional. Craft guilds (or "mysteries") provided religious drama – mystery plays – as part of the celebration of religious and civic festivals, and schools and universities staged classical and neoclassical drama in both Latin and English as part of their curricula. In these forms, drama was established and socially acceptable. Professional theater, in contrast, existed on the margins of society. The acting companies were itinerant; playhouses could be any available space – the great halls of the aristocracy, town squares, civic halls, inn yards, fair booths, or open fields – and income was sporadic, dependent on the passing of the hat or on the bounty of local patrons. The actors, moreover, were considered little better than vagabonds, constantly in danger of arrest or expulsion.

In the late 1560s and 1570s, however, English professional theater began to gain respectability. Wealthy aristocrats fond of drama – the Lord Admiral, for example, or the Lord Chamberlain – took acting companies under their protection so that the players technically became members of their households and were no longer subject to arrest as homeless or masterless men. Permanent theaters were first built at this time as well, allowing the companies to control and charge for entry to their performances.

Shakespeare's livelihood, and the stunning artistic explosion in which he participated, depended on pragmatic and architectural effort. Professional theater requires ways to restrict access to its offerings; if it does not, and admission fees cannot be charged, the actors do not get paid, the costumes go to a pawnbroker, and there is no such thing as a professional, ongoing theatrical tradition. The answer to that economic need arrived in the late 1560s and 1570s with the creation of the so-called public or amphitheater playhouse. Recent discoveries indicate that the precursor of the Globe playhouse in London (where Shakespeare's mature plays were presented) and the Rose theater (which presented Christopher Marlowe's plays and some of Shakespeare's earliest ones) was the Red Lion theater of 1567.

Extensive parts of the foundations of the Rose theater, apparently the fourth public theater to be built, were uncovered in 1989. A few years later, a much smaller portion of the second Globe (rebuilt after the first burned in 1613) was located. The remains of the Rose indicate that it originally (1587) had a rather small "thrust" stage that tapered into the open area from which a standing audience, the "groundlings," watched. The stage was approximately 25 feet wide at the front, more than 36 feet wide at the back, and about 16½ feet deep; it was placed at the northern end of a north-south axis, presumably to maximize the amount of light falling on the stage during the spring-summer playing season. In early 1592, the Rose's owner, Philip Henslowe, paid to renovate and expand his theater; the new stage was at least 18 feet deep, perhaps more if the stage boards projected out over the newly laid brick foundations. The seating area also increased, but both theater and stage remained relatively small compared to the rectangular stage at the Fortune (1600), over 40 feet wide and supposedly based upon the Globe. The Globe building may have been as much as 100 feet in diameter, while the Rose's diameter was about 72 feet. Both theaters were irregular polygons, multistoried, with areas for the groundlings, and with a covered gallery that seated perhaps 2,200 (Rose) or 3,000 (Globe) very crowded spectators.

These theaters might have been about half full on any given day, though the audiences were larger on holidays or when a play was advertised, as old and new were, through printed playbills posted around London. The metropolitan area's late-Tudor, early-Stuart population (circa 1590–1620) has been estimated at about 150,000 to 250,000. It has been supposed that in the mid-1590s there were about 15,000 spectators per week at the public theaters; thus, as many as 10 percent of the local population went to the theater regularly. Consequently, the theaters' repertories – the plays available for this experienced and frequent audience – had to change often: in the month between September 15 and October 15, 1595, for instance, the Lord Admiral's Men performed twenty-eight times in eighteen different plays.

Since natural light illuminated the amphitheaters' stages, performances began between noon and two o'clock and ran without a break for two or three hours. They often concluded with a jig, a fencing display, or some other nondramatic exhibition. Weather conditions determined the season for the amphitheaters: plays were performed every day (including Sundays, sometimes, to clerical dismay) except during Lent – the forty days before Easter – or periods of plague, or sometimes during the summer months when law courts were not in session and the most affluent members of the audience were not in London.

To a modern theatergoer, an amphitheater stage like that of the Rose or Globe would appear an unfamiliar mixture of plainness and elaborate decoration. Much of the structure was carved or painted, sometimes to imitate marble; elsewhere, as under the canopy projecting over the stage, to represent the stars and the zodiac. Appropriate painted canvas pictures (of Jerusalem, for example, if the play was set in that city) were apparently hung on the wall behind the acting area, and tragedies were accompanied by black hangings, presumably something like crepe festoons or bunting. Although these theaters did not employ what we would call scenery, early modern spectators saw numerous large props, such as the "bar" at which a prisoner stood during a trial, the "mossy bank" where lovers reclined, an arbor for amorous conversation, a chariot, gallows, tables, trees, beds, thrones, writing desks, and so forth. Audiences might learn a scene's location from a sign (reading "Athens," for example) carried across the stage (as in Bertolt Brecht's twentieth-century productions). Equally captivating (and equally irritating to the theater's enemies) were the rich costumes and personal props the actors used: the most valuable items in the surviving theatrical inventories are the swords, gowns, robes, crowns, and other items worn or carried by the performers.

Magic appealed to Shakespeare's audiences as much as it does to us today, and the theater exploited many deceptive and spectacular devices. A winch in the loft above the stage, called "the heavens," could lower and raise actors playing gods, goddesses, and other supernatural figures to and from the main acting area, just as one or more trapdoors permitted entrances and exits to and from the area, called "hell," beneath the stage. Actors wore elementary makeup such as wigs, false beards, and face paint, and they employed pigs' bladders filled with animal blood to make wounds seem more real. They had rudimentary but effective ways of pretending to behead or hang a person. Supernumeraries (stagehands or actors not needed in a particular scene) could make thunder sounds (by shaking a metal sheet or rolling an iron ball down a chute) and show lightning (by blowing inflammable resin through tubes into a flame). Elaborate fireworks enhanced the effects of dragons flying through the air or imitated such celestial phenomena as comets, shooting stars, and multiple suns. Horses' hoofbeats, bells (located perhaps in the tower above the stage), trumpets and drums, clocks, cannon shots and gunshots, and the like were common sound effects. And the music of viols, cornets, oboes, and recorders was a regular feature of theatrical performances.

For two relatively brief spans, from the late 1570s to 1590 and from 1599 to 1614, the amphitheaters competed with the so-called private, or indoor, theaters, which originated as, or later represented themselves as, educational institutions training boys as singers for church services and court performances. These indoor theaters had two features that were distinct from the amphitheaters': their personnel and their playing spaces. The amphitheaters' adult companies included both adult men, who played the male roles, and boys, who played the female roles; the private, or indoor, theater companies, on the other hand, were entirely composed of boys aged about eight to sixteen, who were, or could pretend to be, candidates for singers in a church or a royal boys' choir. (Until 1660, professional theatrical companies included no women.) The playing space would appear much more familiar to modern audiences than the long-vanished amphitheaters; the later indoor theaters were, in fact, the ancestors of the typical modern theater. They were enclosed spaces, usually rectangular, with the stage filling one end of the rectangle and the audience arrayed in seats or benches across (and sometimes lining) the building's longer axis. These spaces staged plays less frequently than the public theaters (perhaps only once a week) and held far fewer spectators than the amphitheaters: about 200 to 600, as opposed to 2,500 or more. Fewer patrons mean a smaller gross income, unless each pays more. Not surprisingly, then, private theaters charged higher prices than the amphitheaters, probably sixpence, as opposed to a penny for the cheapest entry to the amphitheaters.

Protected from the weather, the indoor theaters presented plays later in the day than the amphitheaters, and used artificial illumination – candles in sconces or candelabra. But candles melt and need replacing, snuffing, and trimming, and these practical requirements may have been part of the reason the indoor theaters introduced breaks in the performance, the intermission so dear to the hearts of theatergoers and to the pocketbooks of theater concessionaires ever since. Whether motivated by the need to tend to the candles or by the entrepreneurs' wish to sell oranges and liquor, or both, the indoor theaters eventually established the modern convention of noncontinuous performance. In the early modern "private" theater, musical performances apparently filled the intermissions, which in Stuart theater jargon seem to have been called "acts."

At the end of the first decade of the seventeenth century, the distinction between public amphitheaters and private indoor companies ceased. For various cultural, political, and economic reasons, individual companies gained control of both the public, open-air theaters and the indoor ones, and companies mixing adult men and boys took over the formerly "private" theaters. Despite the death of the boys' companies and of their highly innovative theaters (for which such luminous playwrights as Ben Jonson, George Chapman, and John Marston wrote), their playing spaces and conventions had an immense impact on subsequent plays: not merely for the intervals (which stressed the artistic and architectonic importance of "acts"), but also because they introduced political and social satire as a popular dramatic ingredient, even in tragedy, and a wider range of actorly effects, encouraged by the more intimate playing spaces.

Even the briefest sketch of the Shakespearean theatrical world would be incomplete without some comment on the social and cultural dimensions of theaters and playing in the period. In an intensely hierarchical and status-conscious society, professional actors and their ventures had hardly any respectability; as we have indicated, to protect themselves against laws designed to curb vagabondage and the increase of masterless men, actors resorted to the near-fiction that they were the servants of noble masters and wore their distinctive livery. Hence the company for which Shakespeare wrote in the 1590s that called itself the Lord Chamberlain's Men and pretended that the public, money-getting performances were in fact rehearsals for private performances before that high court official. From 1598, the Privy Council had licensed theatrical companies, and after 1603, with the accession of King James I, the companies gained explicit royal protection, just as the Queen's Men had for a time under Queen Elizabeth. The Chamberlain's Men became the King's Men, and the other companies were patronized by other members of the royal family.

These designations were legal fictions that half-concealed an important economic and social development, the evolution away from the theater's organization on the model of the guild, a self-regulating confraternity of individual artisans, into a proto-capitalist organization. Shakespeare's company became a joint-stock company, where persons who supplied capital and, in some cases, such as Shakespeare's, capital and talent, employed themselves and others in earning a return on that capital. This development meant that actors and theater companies were outside both the traditional guild structures, which required some form of civic or royal charter, and the feudal household organization of master-and-servant. This anomalous, maverick social and economic condition made theater companies practically unruly and potentially even dangerous; consequently, numerous official bodies – including the London metropolitan and ecclesiastical authorities as well as, occasionally, the royal court itself – tried, without much success, to control and even to disband them.

Public officials had good reason to want to close the theaters: they were attractive nuisances – they drew often-riotous crowds, they were always noisy, and they could be politically offensive and socially insubordinate. Until the Civil War, however, antitheatrical forces failed to shut down professional theater, for many reasons – limited surveillance and few police powers, tensions or outright hostilities among the agencies that sought to check or channel theatrical activity, and lack of clear policies for control. Another reason must have been the theaters' undeniable popularity. Curtailing any activity enjoyed by such a substantial percentage of the population was difficult, as various Roman emperors attempting to limit circuses had learned, and the Tudor-Stuart audience was not merely large, it was socially diverse and included women. The prevalence of public entertainment in this period has been underestimated. In fact, fairs, holidays, games, sporting events, the equivalent of modern parades, freak shows, and street exhibitions all abounded, but the theater was the most widely and frequently available entertainment to which people of every class had access. That fact helps account both for its quantity and for the fear and anger it aroused.

Books About Shakespeare's Theater

Useful scholarly studies of theatrical life in Shakespeare's day include: G. E. Bentley, *The Jacobean and Caroline Stage,* 7 vols. (1941–68), and the same author's *The Professions of Dramatist and Player in Shakespeare's Time, 1590–1642* (1986); Julian Bowsher, *The Rose Theatre: An Archaeological Discovery* (1998); E. K. Chambers, *The Elizabethan Stage,* 4 vols. (1923); Christine Eccles, *The Rose Theatre* (1990); R. A. Foakes, *Illustrations of the English Stage, 1580–1642* (1985); Andrew Gurr, *The Shakespearean Stage, 1574–1642,* 3rd ed. (1992), and the same author's *Playgoing in Shakespeare's London,* 2nd ed. (1996); Roslyn Lander Knutson, *Playing Companies and Commerce in Shakespeare's Time* (2001); Edwin Nungezer, *A Dictionary of Actors* (1929); Carol Chillington Rutter, ed., *Documents of the Rose Playhouse* (1984); Tiffany Stern, *Documents of Performance in Early Modern England* (2009); Glynne Wickham, Herbert Berry, and William Ingram, *English Professional Theatre, 1530–1660* (2009).

William Shakespeare of Stratford-upon-Avon, Gentleman

Many people have said that we know very little about William Shakespeare's life – pinheads and postcards are often mentioned as appropriately tiny surfaces on which to record the available information. More imaginatively and perhaps more correctly, Ralph Waldo Emerson wrote, "Shakespeare is the only biographer of Shakespeare. . . . So far from Shakespeare's being the least known, he is the one person in all modern history fully known to us."

In fact, we know more about Shakespeare's life than we do about almost any other English writer's of his era. His last will and testament (dated March 25, 1616) survives, as do numerous legal contracts and court documents involving Shakespeare as principal or witness, and parish records in Stratford and London. Shakespeare appears quite often in official records of King James's royal court, and of course Shakespeare's name appears on numerous title pages and in the written and recorded words of his literary contemporaries Robert Greene, Henry Chettle, Francis Meres, John Davies of Hereford, Ben Jonson, and many others. Indeed, if we make due allowance for the bloating of modern, run-of-the-mill bureaucratic records, more information has survived over the past four hundred years about William Shakespeare of Stratford-upon-Avon, Warwickshire, than is likely to survive in the next four hundred years about any reader of these words.

What we do not have are entire categories of information – Shakespeare's private letters or diaries, drafts and revisions of poems and plays, critical prefaces or essays, commendatory verse for other writers' works, or instructions guiding his fellow actors in their performances, for instance – that we imagine would help us understand and appreciate his surviving writings. For all we know, many such data never existed as written records. Many literary and theatrical critics, not knowing what might once have existed, more or less cheerfully accept the situation; some even make a theoretical virtue of it by claiming that such data are irrelevant to understanding and interpreting the plays and poems.

So, what do we know about William Shakespeare, the man responsible for thirty-seven or perhaps more plays, more than 150 sonnets, two lengthy narrative poems, and some shorter poems?

While many families by the name of Shakespeare (or some variant spelling) can be identified in the English Midlands as far back as the twelfth century, it seems likely that the dramatist's grandfather, Richard, moved to Snitterfield, a town not far from Stratford-upon-Avon, sometime before 1529. In Snitterfield, Richard Shakespeare leased farmland from the very wealthy Robert Arden. By 1552, Richard's son John had moved to a large house on Henley Street in Stratford-upon-Avon, the house that stands today as "The Birthplace." In Stratford, John Shakespeare traded as a glover, dealt in wool, and lent money at interest; he also served in a variety of civic posts, including "High Bailiff," the municipality's equivalent of mayor. In 1557, he married Robert Arden's youngest daughter, Mary. Mary and John had four sons – William was the oldest – and four daughters, of whom only Joan outlived her most celebrated sibling. William was baptized (an event entered in the Stratford parish church records) on April 26, 1564, and it has become customary, without any good factual support, to suppose he was born on April 23, which happens to be the feast day of Saint George, patron saint of England, and is also the date on which Shakespeare died, in 1616. Shakespeare married Anne Hathaway in 1582, when he was eighteen and she was twenty-six; their first child was born five months later. It has been generally assumed that the marriage was enforced and subsequently unhappy, but these are only assumptions; it has been estimated, for instance, that up to one-third of Elizabethan brides were pregnant when they married. Anne and William Shakespeare had three children: Susanna, who married a prominent local physician, John Hall; and the twins Hamnet, who died young in 1596, and Judith, who married Thomas Quiney – apparently a rather shady individual. The name Hamnet was unusual but not unique: he and his twin sister were named for their godparents, Shakespeare's neighbors Hamnet and Judith Sadler. Shakespeare's father died in 1601 (the year of *Hamlet*), and Mary Arden Shakespeare died in 1608 (the year of *Coriolanus*). William Shakespeare's last surviving direct descendant was his granddaughter Elizabeth Hall, who died in 1670.

Between the birth of the twins in 1585 and a clear reference to Shakespeare as a practicing London dramatist in Robert Greene's sensationalizing, satiric pamphlet, *Greene's*

Groatsworth of Wit (1592), there is no record of where William Shakespeare was or what he was doing. These seven so-called lost years have been imaginatively filled by scholars and other students of Shakespeare: some think he traveled to Italy, or fought in the Low Countries, or studied law or medicine, or worked as an apprentice actor/writer, and so on to even more fanciful possibilities. Whatever the biographical facts for those "lost" years, Greene's nasty remarks in 1592 testify to professional envy and to the fact that Shakespeare already had a successful career in London. Speaking to his fellow playwrights, Greene warns both generally and specifically:

> . . . trust them [actors] not: for there is an upstart crow, beautified with our feathers, that with his tiger's heart wrapped in a player's hide supposes he is as well able to bombast out a blank verse as the best of you; and being an absolute Johannes Factotum, is in his own conceit the only Shake-scene in a country.

The passage mimics a line from *3 Henry VI* (hence the play must have been performed before Greene wrote) and seems to say that "Shake-scene" is both actor and playwright, a jack-of-all-trades. That same year, Henry Chettle protested Greene's remarks in *Kind-Heart's Dream*, and each of the next two years saw the publication of poems – *Venus and Adonis* and *Lucrece,* respectively – publicly ascribed to (and dedicated by) Shakespeare. Early in 1595 he was named as one of the senior members of a prominent acting company, the Lord Chamberlain's Men, when they received payment for court performances during the 1594 Christmas season.

Clearly, Shakespeare had achieved both success and reputation in London. In 1596, upon Shakespeare's application, the College of Arms granted his father the now-familiar coat of arms he had taken the first steps to obtain almost twenty years before, and in 1598, John's son – now permitted to call himself "gentleman" – took a 10 percent share in the new Globe playhouse. In 1597, he bought a substantial bourgeois house, called New Place, in Stratford – the garden remains, but Shakespeare's house, several times rebuilt, was torn down in 1759 – and over the next few years Shakespeare spent large sums buying land and making other investments in the town and its environs. Though he worked in London, his family remained in Stratford, and he seems always to have considered Stratford the home he would eventually return to. Something approaching a disinterested appreciation of Shakespeare's popular and professional status appears in Francis Meres's *Palladis Tamia* (1598), a not especially imaginative and perhaps therefore persuasive record of literary reputations. Reviewing contemporary English writers, Meres lists the titles of many of Shakespeare's plays, including one not now known, *Love's Labor's Won*, and praises his "mellifluous & hony-tongued" "sugred Sonnets," which were then circulating in manuscript (they were first collected in 1609). Meres describes Shakespeare as "one of the best" English playwrights of both comedy and tragedy. In *Remains . . . Concerning Britain* (1605), William Camden – a more authoritative source than the imitative Meres – calls Shakespeare one of the "most pregnant witts of these our times" and joins him with such writers as Chapman, Daniel, Jonson, Marston, and Spenser. During the first decades of the seventeenth century, publishers began to attribute numerous play quartos, including some non-Shakespearean ones, to Shakespeare, either by name or initials, and we may assume that they deemed Shakespeare's name and supposed authorship, true or false, commercially attractive.

For the next ten years or so, various records show Shakespeare's dual career as playwright and man of the theater in London, and as an important local figure in Stratford. In 1608–9 his acting company – designated the "King's Men" soon after King James had succeeded Queen Elizabeth in 1603 – rented, refurbished, and opened a small interior playing space, the Blackfriars theater, in London, and Shakespeare was once again listed as a substantial sharer in the group of proprietors of the playhouse. By May 11, 1612, however, he describes himself as a Stratford resident in a London lawsuit – an indication that he had withdrawn from day-to-day professional activity and returned to the town where he had always had his main financial interests. When Shakespeare bought a substantial residential building in London, the Blackfriars Gatehouse, close to the theater of the same name, on March 10, 1613, he is recorded as William Shakespeare "of Stratford upon Avon in the county of Warwick, gentleman," and he named several London residents as the building's trustees. Still, he continued to participate in theatrical activity: when the new Earl of Rutland needed an allegorical design to bear as a shield, or *impresa*, at the celebration of King James's Accession Day, March 24, 1613, the earl's accountant recorded a payment of 44 shillings to Shakespeare for the device with its motto.

For the last few years of his life, Shakespeare evidently concentrated his activities in the town of his birth. Most of the final records concern business transactions in Stratford, ending with the notation of his death on April 23, 1616, and burial in Holy Trinity Church, Stratford-upon-Avon.

The Question of Authorship

The history of ascribing Shakespeare's plays (the poems do not come up so often) to someone else began, as it continues, peculiarly. The earliest published claim that someone else wrote Shakespeare's plays appeared in an 1856 article by Delia Bacon in the American journal *Putnam's Monthly* – although an Englishman, Thomas Wilmot, had shared his doubts in private (even secretive) conversations with friends near the end of the eighteenth century. Bacon's was a sad personal history that ended in madness and poverty, but the year after her article, she published, with great difficulty and the bemused assistance of Nathaniel Hawthorne (then United States Consul in Liverpool, England), her *Philosophy of the Plays of Shakspere Unfolded.* This huge, ornately written, confusing farrago is almost unreadable; sometimes its intents, to say nothing of its arguments, disappear entirely beneath near-raving, ecstatic writing. Tumbled in with much supposed "philosophy" appear the claims that Francis Bacon (from whom Delia Bacon eventually claimed descent), Walter Ralegh, and several other contemporaries of Shakespeare's had written the plays. The book had little impact except as a ridiculed curiosity.

Once proposed, however, the issue gained momentum among people whose conviction was the greater in proportion to their ignorance of sixteenth- and seventeenth-century English literature, history, and society. Another American amateur, Catharine F. Ashmead Windle, made the next influential contribution to the cause when she published *Report to the British Museum* (1882), wherein she promised to open "the Cipher of Francis Bacon," though what she mostly offers, in the words of S. Schoenbaum, is "demented allegorizing." An entire new cottage industry grew from Windle's suggestion that the texts contain hidden, cryptographically discoverable ciphers – "clues" – to their authorship; and today there are not only books devoted to the putative ciphers, but also pamphlets, journals, and newsletters.

Although Baconians have led the pack of those seeking a substitute Shakespeare, in *"Shakespeare" Identified* (1920), J. Thomas Looney became the first published "Oxfordian" when he proposed Edward de Vere, seventeenth earl of Oxford, as the secret author of Shakespeare's plays. Also for Oxford and his "authorship" there are today dedicated societies, articles, journals, and books. Less popular candidates – Queen Elizabeth and Christopher Marlowe among them – have had adherents, but the movement seems to have divided into two main contending factions, Baconian and Oxfordian. (For further details on all the candidates for "Shakespeare," see S. Schoenbaum, *Shakespeare's Lives,* 2nd ed., 1991.)

The Baconians, the Oxfordians, and supporters of other candidates have one trait in common – they are snobs.

Every pro-Bacon or pro-Oxford tract sooner or later claims that the historical William Shakespeare of Stratford-upon-Avon could not have written the plays because he could not have had the training, the university education, the experience, and indeed the imagination or background their author supposedly possessed. Only a learned genius like Bacon or an aristocrat like Oxford could have written such fine plays. (As it happens, lucky male children of the middle class had access to better education than most aristocrats in Elizabethan England – and Oxford was not particularly well educated.) Shakespeare received in the Stratford grammar school a formal education that would daunt many college graduates today; and popular rival playwrights such as the very learned Ben Jonson and George Chapman, both of whom also lacked university training, achieved great artistic success without being taken as Bacon or Oxford.

Besides snobbery, one other quality characterizes the authorship controversy: lack of evidence. A great deal of testimony from Shakespeare's time shows that Shakespeare wrote Shakespeare's plays and that his contemporaries recognized them as distinctive and distinctly superior. (Some of that contemporary evidence is collected in E. K. Chambers, *William Shakespeare: A Study of Facts and Problems*, 2 vols., 1930.) Since that testimony comes from Shakespeare's enemies and theatrical competitors as well as from his coworkers and from the Elizabethan equivalent of literary journalists, it seems unlikely that, if any of these sources had known he was a fraud, they would have failed to record that fact.

Books About Shakespeare's Life

The following books provide scholarly, documented accounts of Shakespeare's life: G. E. Bentley, *Shakespeare: A Biographical Handbook* (1961); E. K. Chambers, *William Shakespeare: A Study of Facts and Problems,* 2 vols. (1930); S. Schoenbaum, *William Shakespeare: A Compact Documentary Life* (1977), and the same author's *Shakespeare's*

Lives, 2nd ed. (1991); and James Shapiro, *Contested Will: Who Wrote Shakespeare?* (2010). Many scholarly editions of Shakespeare's complete works print brief compilations of essential dates and events. References to Shakespeare's works up to 1700 are collected in C. M. Ingleby et al., *Shakespeare Allusion-Book,* rev. ed., 2 vols. (1932).

The Texts of Shakespeare

As far as we know, only one manuscript conceivably in Shakespeare's own hand may (and even this is much disputed) exist: a few pages of a play called *Sir Thomas More*, which apparently was never performed. What we do have, as later readers, performers, scholars, students, are printed texts. The earliest of these survive in two forms: quartos and folios. Quartos (from the Latin for "four") are small books, printed on sheets of paper that were then folded twice, to make four leaves or eight pages. When these were bound together, the result was a squarish, eminently portable volume that sold for the relatively small sum of sixpence (translating in modern terms to about $5). In folios, on the other hand, the sheets are folded only once, in half, producing large, impressive volumes taller than they are wide. This was the format for important works of philosophy, science, theology, and literature (the major precedent for a folio Shakespeare was Ben Jonson's *Works*, 1616). The decision to print the works of a popular playwright in folio is an indication of how far up on the social scale the theatrical profession had come during Shakespeare's lifetime. The Shakespeare folio was an expensive book, selling for between fifteen and eighteen shillings, depending on the binding (in modern terms, from about $150 to $180). Twenty Shakespeare plays of the thirty-seven that survive first appeared in quarto, seventeen of which appeared during Shakespeare's lifetime; the rest of the plays are found only in folio.

The First Folio was published in 1623, seven years after Shakespeare's death, and was authorized by his fellow actors, the co-owners of the King's Men. This publication was certainly a mark of the company's enormous respect for Shakespeare; but it was also a way of turning the old plays, most of which were no longer current in the playhouse, into ready money (the folio includes only Shakespeare's plays, not his sonnets or other nondramatic verse). Whatever the motives behind the publication of the folio, the texts it preserves constitute the basis for almost all later editions of the playwright's works. The texts, however, differ from those of the earlier quartos, sometimes in minor respects but often significantly – most strikingly in the two texts of *King Lear*, but also in important ways in *Hamlet*, *Othello*, and *Troilus and Cressida*. (The variants are recorded in the textual notes to each play.) The differences in these texts represent, in a sense, the essence of theater: the texts of the plays were initially not intended for publication. They were scripts, designed for the actors to perform – the principal life of the play at this period was in performance. And it follows that in Shakespeare's theater the playwright typically had no say either in how his play was performed or in the disposition of his text – he was an employee of the company. The authoritative figures in the theatrical enterprise were the shareholders in the company, who were for the most part the major actors. They decided what plays were to be done; they hired the playwright and often gave him an outline of the play they wanted him to write. Often, too, the play was a collaboration: the company would retain a group of writers and parcel out the scenes among them. The resulting script was then the property of the company, and the actors would revise it as they saw fit during the course of putting it onstage. The resulting text belonged to the company. The playwright had no rights in it once he had been paid. (This system survives largely intact in the movie industry, and most of the playwrights of Shakespeare's time were as anonymous as most screenwriters are today.) The script could also, of course, continue to change as the tastes of audiences and the requirements of the actors changed. Many – perhaps most – plays were revised when they were reintroduced after any substantial absence from the repertory, or when they were performed by a company different from the one that originally commissioned the play.

Shakespeare was an exceptional figure in this world because he was not only a shareholder and actor in his company, but also its leading playwright – he was literally his own boss. He had, moreover, little interest in the publication of his plays, and even those that appeared during his lifetime with the authorization of the company show no signs of any editorial concern on the part of the author. Theater was, for Shakespeare, a fluid and supremely responsive medium – the very opposite of the great classic canonical text that has embodied his works since 1623.

The very fluidity of the original texts, however, has meant that Shakespeare has always had to be edited. Here is an example of how problematic the editorial project inevitably is, a passage from the most famous speech in *Romeo and Juliet*, Juliet's balcony soliloquy beginning "O Romeo, Romeo, wherefore art thou Romeo?" Since the eighteenth century, the standard modern text has read:

> What's Montague? It is nor hand, nor foot,
> Nor arm, nor face, nor any other part
> Belonging to a man. O be some other name!
> What's in a name? That which we call a rose
> By any other name would smell as sweet.
> (II.2.40–44)

Editors have three early texts of this play to work from, two quarto texts and the folio. Here is how the First Quarto (1597) reads:

> Whats *Mountague?* It is nor hand nor foote,
> Nor arme, nor face, nor any other part.
> Whats in a name? That which we call a Rose,
> By any other name would ſmell as ſweet:

Here is the Second Quarto (1599):

> Whats *Mountague?* it is nor hand nor foote,
> Nor arme nor face, ô be ſome other name
> Belonging to a man.
> Whats in a name that which we call a roſe,
> By any other word would ſmell as ſweete,

And here is the First Folio (1623):

> What's *Mountague*? it is nor hand nor foote,
> Nor arme, nor face, O be ſome other name
> Belonging to a man.
> What? in a names that which we call a Roſe,
> By any other word would ſmell as ſweete,

There is in fact no early text that reads as our modern text does – and this is the most famous speech in the play. Instead, we have three quite different texts, all of which are clearly some version of the same speech, but none of which seems to us a final or satisfactory version. The transcendently beautiful passage in modern editions is an editorial invention: editors have succeeded in conflating and revising the three versions into something we recognize as great poetry. Is this what Shakespeare "really" wrote? Who can say? What we can say is that Shakespeare always had performance, not a book, in mind.

Books About the Shakespeare Texts

The standard studies of the printing history of the First Folio are W. W. Greg, *The Shakespeare First Folio* (1955), and Charlton Hinman, *The Printing and Proof-Reading of the First Folio of Shakespeare* (1963). J. K. Walton, *The Quarto Copy for the First Folio of Shakespeare* (1971), is a useful survey of the relation of the quartos to the folio. The second edition of Charlton Hinman's *Norton Facsimile* of the First Folio (1996), with a new introduction by Peter W. M. Blayney, is indispensable. Stanley Wells, Gary Taylor, John Jowett, and William Montgomery, *William Shakespeare: A Textual Companion*, keyed to the Oxford text, gives a comprehensive survey of the editorial situation for all the plays and poems.

Introduction

SHAKESPEARE'S OVERWHELMING study of the tragedy of old age and the politics of the family has held the stage continuously since its first performance in 1606. In recent years it has rivaled *Hamlet* and *Romeo and Juliet* as the most frequently produced and intensely studied of Shakespeare's tragedies; its analysis of the disintegration of the closest family ties, the resentment and violence underlying the most intimate relationships, has seemed to speak to peculiarly modern concerns. In Shakespeare's own time it spoke as well to much larger political issues: the responsibilities of kingship, the continuity of rule, the unity of the commonwealth, and perhaps most troubling of all, the profound tenuousness of a patriarchal social order – of the assumption that the model for the commonwealth was the family, and that on all levels of society, father was king. Indeed, even overtly political tragedy, for Shakespeare, invariably starts in the family. It is Richard II's behavior toward his uncles and cousins that prompts the rebellion that deposes him; the tragedy of Hamlet begins with fratricide and incest, and takes shape around the complex relations of parents and children; Macbeth, assassinating Duncan at the urging of his wife, is murdering his first cousin; Lear's tragedy is from beginning to end a family matter. It is to the point that when James I came to the English throne in 1603, there was a fully constituted royal family at the center of English society for the first time since the death of Henry VIII. The first recorded performance of *King Lear*, on December 26, 1606, was at Whitehall Palace before King James – though the play seems to have been written in the previous year, the court performance may well have been the first, since plague had closed the public theaters for the season. If this is the case, Shakespeare's play began its life with Britain's royal patriarch at the center of its audience.

But the opening scene hardly mirrors the Jacobean court. Though the story of Lear comes from the chronicles of ancient Britain, the action belongs more to the world of legend than history. Lear's court initially seems like a fairy-tale world, where momentous decisions are determined by trifles. The opening moments of the play invite us not to take the action seriously. The declarations of love Lear demands from his three daughters are to be performances, set pieces. Nothing apparently depends on them, since the division of the kingdom has already been decided upon – Lear arrives with a map already prepared. His daughters understand perfectly what is required of them; they have only to play their parts. Cordelia, refusing to produce her accolade, is disrupting both a courtly ceremonial and a family game, and it comes as a profound surprise to everyone present. In insisting on her right to silence, she is not only refusing to play, but is changing the rules.

How are we to take this scene? We could say that it is a debate between style and meaning, with Goneril and Regan showing their rhetorical art, and Cordelia, distrusting language, refusing to say what she does not believe. The older sisters' performances purport to be deeds, acts of homage to the king their father; but Cordelia objects that words are not deeds. From Goneril and Regan's perspective, these performances are noble ceremonies, hyperbolic and therefore appropriate responses to their royal father; from Cordelia's, they are merely specious shows, cheapening the king because they are inherently dishonest. If we look at the scene this way, it constitutes a debate between rhetoricians and plain-speakers, and it includes a good deal of the Elizabethan distrust of the theater as well – the fear that its representations will be taken for, and will thereby undermine or subvert, reality. Significantly here, it is the villains who are the performers.

We could look at the scene another way and say that the three sisters are being asked to sign a loyalty oath. Goneril and Regan agree to it because they are aware that the oath is really meaningless, and Cordelia refuses for exactly the same reason: because she too is aware that the oath is meaningless – the same perceptions can produce opposite actions, and motives for action are incalculable. The moral implications of the scene are immensely complicated because the issues are so trifling. Is Lear at fault for demanding the performance, for requiring the oath? As it turns out, he is, but we can imagine a different outcome, in which the willing adherence to the honorable forms of ceremonial behavior is seen as the essence of civilized society. These are precisely the values that Hamlet is nostalgic for, the old chivalric world, the world Macbeth destroys with his murder of Duncan. Whether Lear is at fault or not is almost beside the point: the point, as the scene proceeds, is much more schematic, and reminds us of Macbeth's world of paradoxes. The good daughter cannot express her love while the bad daughters are believed; speech is lying and silence is truth; the richest reality is nothing – what Cordelia says, what her dowry is.

These issues relate to the larger question of the nature of power. In this scene about royalty and its dependencies, what constitutes power? In the case of the sisters, it is the ability to speak and please the king. The king's power is, to begin with, the power to bestow the monarchy. But Lear thinks of it in much less practical and more metaphysical ways, as the power of his senses –

> Hence, and avoid my sight! (I.1.122)*

– and even more significantly, as the power of his language. Kent, urging Lear to rescind his decree, has sought "To come between our sentence and our power": a *sentence*, the crucial unit of structured language, is also the exercise of judicial authority. In our legal system, the full

* Citations are to the folio text.

power of the law is still imposed by that word "sentence." To punish criminals, we sentence them.

What Lear does *not* conceive his power to be is his position, the mere fact that he is king. But this, of course, is the sole source of his power, and he makes clear the way the drama is to move by resigning his office but nevertheless undertaking to retain "The name, and all th' addition to a king" (134). A question the play examines most intensely is what the name of king is – is it another nothing? What "addition" can a nothing have – what more than nothing is a nothing entitled to? And what is authority, which Kent sees in the face of the mad Lear? Can there be authority without power? What are the bases of judgment, essential for effective government? This question is central to *Macbeth*, too, as King Duncan observes of the thane who has betrayed him: "There's no art / To find the mind's construction in the face" (I.4.11–12).

Clearly the basis of judgment is not loyalty oaths. Even the victorious sisters realize how foolish Lear has been, observing, "with what poor judgment he hath now cast [Cordelia] off appears too grossly" (I.1.290–91). More important is their observation that "he hath ever but slenderly known himself" (292–93); it implies that Lear's behavior is not simply a function of old age, but is both characteristic and at the heart of the play's disruptions. A king without self-knowledge is notoriously a danger to the commonwealth. But is Lear really responsible for the ensuing tragedy? How far could even the best of kings contain the villainy of Goneril, Regan, Cornwall, Edmund? Could Cordelia do so?

Moreover, though it is Kent who initially objects to Lear's bad judgment, only the villains assume that it renders him unfit to rule. In fact, elsewhere in the play Lear is referred to not as blind, foolish, irascible, self-centered, tyrannical, but as *kind* – Kent deplores "the hard rein which both of them hath borne / Against the old kind king . . ." (III.1.19–20). Lear on himself, "So kind a father!" (I.5.32), is presumably to be taken ironically, but his later characterization of himself, "Your old kind father, whose frank heart gave all" (III.4.20), is, objectively, true, though of course not the whole truth. When Richard Burbage, the leading tragedian of Shakespeare's company, died in 1619, his elegy listed the roles that made him famous:

> No more young Hamlet, old Hieronymo,
> Kind Lear, the grievèd Moor . . .*

The point here is not only that Lear is entitled to respect and pity, but even more significantly, that in a monarchy based on a philosophy of Divine Right, a bad king is still the king. This is no doubt why King James liked this play about the extreme precariousness of kingship enough to have it performed at court. The play was, in this respect, for its original audiences, both politically conservative and basically sentimental. Modern audiences and critics who focus on Lear's irrationality and incompetence have adopted the point of view of the villains.

As Lear's plot derives from both ancient history and Jacobean politics, the parallel plot of Gloucester and his good and bad sons derives from contemporary romance. Shakespeare took the story from Sir Philip Sidney's immensely popular novel *Arcadia*, written in the 1580s, and an instant classic – by 1605 it had already gone through four editions. Gloucester's tragedy provides a running commentary on that of Lear and his daughters, but it also has its own momentum. Modern audiences find the casualness of Gloucester's attitude to Edmund's bastardy in the opening exchange with Kent at least disconcerting, if not reprehensible; but illegitimacy was a commonplace fact of Shakespeare's England, as it must be of any society without reliable methods of birth control, and though illegitimate children were barred from the line of succession and the inheritance of landed estates, no stigma was attached to the fact of bastardy itself. Noblemen freely

* *Shakespeare Allusion Book,* John Munro, ed. (London: Oxford University Press, 1932), 1:272.

acknowledged their illegitimate children, and often provided handsomely for them, and illegitimacy was no bar to social and political success: Elizabeth's powerful minister the Earl of Leicester was illegitimate, as were, technically, both Elizabeth herself and her predecessor on the throne, Queen Mary I. Edmund complains of his bastardy, etymologizing it (incorrectly) from "base," but it is important to emphasize that he loses nothing on account of it. He is younger than the legitimate son, Edgar, not older, and therefore even if he were not illegitimate, he would be entitled only to whatever his father chooses to give him: under the English law of primogeniture, the eldest son inherits the title, and the bulk of the estate. In fact, Edmund is contemptuous of his father precisely because he makes no distinction between his two sons, but loves and trusts them equally – contemptuous not because Gloucester is blind to the fact that Edmund is a bastard but because he is blind to the fact that he is a villain.

But Edmund is more than a villain. He is in his way the great realist of the play. Invoking Nature as his goddess in a powerful soliloquy at the opening of Act I, scene 2, he defies conventional morality in favor of an ethic of pure self-interest. Shakespeare's contemporaries would have seen him as a Machiavellian figure, and to that extent a conventional stage villain; but what is probably most striking about him for us is the way he analyzes and overturns the idea of nature so central to the largest ethical claims of the play, the idea of nature as a benign and humane force. From Lear's and Cordelia's perspectives, Goneril and Regan are behaving unnaturally; from Edmund's, they are fulfilling nature's law, what we would call the law of the jungle. It is Goneril and Regan who are the play's conventional villains; Edmund is a genuinely subversive figure. He loses in the end, certainly, but so do Lear and Cordelia; and what he introduces into the play is a serious question about the basis of ethical behavior.

The Nature Edmund invokes is anarchic, full of competing claims, not ordered and hierarchical. To acknowledge such a Nature is to acknowledge the reality, force, and validity of the individual will – to acknowledge that all of us have claims that conflict with claims about the deference due to fathers and kings, about the hierarchy of society and what is natural within the family. This is the recognition that Edmund brings into *King Lear* when he invokes Nature as his goddess. It is a Nature that is not the image of divine order, but one in which the strongest and craftiest survive – and when they survive, they then go on to devise claims about Nature that justify their success, claims about hierarchies, natural law and order, the divine right of kings, the sanctity of the father. Edmund is a villain, but if he were ultimately successful he would be indistinguishable from the Lears and Cordelias (and James the Firsts) of Shakespeare's world.

Such concerns may seem to us anachronistic: we tend to believe that for Shakespeare's society the order of nature was a norm, the sanctity of patriarchy unquestionable. But ambivalence about what is natural within the family was built into the very language of Elizabethan England: the alternative term for an illegitimate child was a natural child – it is the legitimate, here, that is unnatural. Edmund raises all the issues that Machiavelli had introduced into Renaissance political discourse, and the fear generated by the figure of the Machiavel in Renaissance England is a measure of how genuinely subversive those issues were. The fact that Edmund must live by his wits, that he is entitled only to what he can gain by his own efforts, actually makes him representative of a large segment of Shakespeare's audience: his situation is not only that of bastards, but of every younger son in a culture that practices primogeniture. Edmund stands, disturbingly, at the center of the society's doubts about itself.

The ease with which Edmund's elder brother, Edgar, Gloucester's legitimate heir, is displaced, is a measure of how forcefully those doubts were felt. Gloucester's whole sense of the beloved Edgar is overturned in an instant by Edmund's deception, as Lear's sense of Cordelia is overturned by a single act of obduracy. At the heart of the play, in both Lear's and Gloucester's families, is a conviction that human nature, even the nature of those closest to us, is essentially unknowable. Doubtless both Gloucester's and Edgar's gullibility are strongly contributing factors in the success of Edmund's schemes, but that gullibility stems precisely from their faith in the essential goodness and honesty of human nature. Would skepticism be sufficient protection against Edmund's villainy?

Once the enabling actions of the opening two scenes have occurred, the tragedy takes shape with extraordinary swiftness. Lear's reduction from monarch to "a poor old man, / As full of grief as age, wretched in both" (II.4.265–66), is complete by the end of Act II, the blinding of Gloucester by the end of Act III. The whole action of the play covers no more than a few weeks. It is not only the speed of this that is notable, but its violence, the abjectness of Lear's misery and madness, the savagery of Gloucester's treatment at the hands of Cornwall, Regan, and Goneril. The savagery is visited, moreover, not only on the characters but on the audience as well: deaths, even murders, take place on Shakespeare's stage in every tragedy, but the blinding of Gloucester is all but unique – the closest parallel, the mutilation of Lavinia in *Titus Andronicus*, takes place offstage.

Along with the violence, the play has a strong erotic element, though it has little to do with the issues of marriage that fill the opening scene –"tell me how much you love me" is what fathers say to children in this play, not what lovers say to each other. The most powerful erotic forces of the play are those of the villains, the adulterous passion of Goneril and Regan for Edmund. It is this that turns the sisters from natural allies to natural enemies. Even so, the play includes no love scenes.

What, then, are the erotics of the opening scene? Burgundy and France have, after all, come to woo Cordelia, but for both, the issue of inheritance is the primary one. There is nothing culturally inappropriate about this: the reason women in early modern cultures are provided with dowries is that men will not marry them otherwise. In patriarchal societies, women are property, and no matter how intelligent, accomplished, charming, or beautiful they may be, the property is essential, and the more property they represent the more desirable they are. Love is not irrelevant to marriage, but neither is it the sole nor even the primary consideration, and it is often represented as what follows from a prosperous marriage, not what brings it about. Lear dividing the kingdom among his three daughters, moreover, is following the dictates of English law: primogeniture applied exclusively to male heirs. If there were only daughters, they inherited equally – Lear's willfulness in the matter is manifested merely in his determination to give Cordelia a better portion than her sisters.

Why then does Cordelia become more attractive to the King of France when she is dowryless, and out of favor with her father? This, in fact, is the romance element in the plot: the love interest is represented as both chivalric and quixotic. Of course, France's romantic passion can also be seen cynically (or realistically) as representing basically an investment. The French king supporting, indeed, urging, an invasion of England by an army led by his wife on behalf of his father-in-law is hardly disinterested. France is not concerned solely to get Lear in out of the rain; to rescue Lear means repossessing at least Cordelia's original third of the kingdom, and perhaps all of it. Cordelia is a gamble, but in all the sources the gamble pays off handsomely: in Holinshed's *Chronicles*, from which Shakespeare took his history, Cordelia's army wins, Lear retrieves his throne, and Cordelia succeeds him. The surprise for a Jacobean audience would have been that in Shakespeare the gamble fails.

The parallel between Lear and Gloucester plays itself out as a double tragedy with two quite different morals. Both men are attended by the figures they have decisively rejected, either in disguise, like Kent and Edgar, or in the plain-speaking Fool, a surrogate Cordelia. Edgar leads his blind father out of despair through a little staged miracle, the extraordinary imagined fall from Dover Cliff in IV.5. But the resulting patience and acceptance lead to nothing but death, without even the recognition and reconciliation scene we have surely been primed to expect – and which is an essential element of the story in Shakespeare's source for the Gloucester plot, the episode of the Paphlagonian king in Sidney's *Arcadia* (Book 2, Chapter 10). In Sidney, the reconciliation has taken place even before the story is recounted, and is, in a sense, a determining condition of the story. Shakespeare's Edgar, almost at the play's end, merely reports that at the moment of Gloucester's death he did finally reveal his identity – the shock of recognition, in fact, is what killed Gloucester. But the announcement comes almost as an afterthought, the tying up of a loose end.

Gloucester is effectively abandoned by the play. His tragedy is framed, moreover, with a simplistic moral. Edgar, confronting Edmund at the end, says,

> The gods are just, and of our pleasant vices [Q: virtues]
> Make instruments to plague us.
> The dark and vicious place where thee he got
> Cost him his eyes.
>
> (V.3.163–66)

Edmund agrees: "Thou'st spoken right; 'tis true. / The wheel is come full circle." But as a summation of Gloucester's tragedy, the lines seem singularly obtuse: Gloucester dies blaming his gullibility and imperceptiveness; he never gives any sign of regret for his youthful adultery. We will be especially unpersuaded by Edgar's conviction of the economy of divine justice if we think of Cordelia's fate, and even of Lear's, which seem more appropriately summed up with Gloucester's own cosmic epigram,

> As flies to wanton boys are we to th' gods:
> They kill us for their sport.
>
> (IV.1.36–37)

Tragedy may be a moralizing form, but it is not an equitable one: the innocent invariably suffer with the guilty, and often more than the guilty. If tragedy has a moral, it is surely that we *do not* get what we deserve. We might contrast the sense Edgar makes of his tragedy with the sense Cordelia, stoical in defeat, makes of hers: "We are not the first / Who with best meaning have incurred the worst" (V.3.3–4).

In the tragedy of Lear and Cordelia, the moral is obscure but the suffering and awareness are the measures of value. Renaissance philosophy and theology almost without exception took the position of Lear and Cordelia. Edgar's notion of cosmic justice would have been considered to be like a belief in horoscopes, naive and simplistic. Providence works on far too vast a scale for individual suffering to be included in it – the heavens do not provide comfort: that one must make for oneself. Virtue, proverbial wisdom tells us, is its own reward: the virtuous gain nothing but the thing itself, the knowledge that they are virtuous. This is not a philosophy designed to produce happy endings.

Renaissance Christianity was not a cozy or friendly faith; whether Protestant or Catholic, the church was fierce and uncompromising, not the welcoming mother one could always return to, but an omnipotent and largely disapproving father. The notion of a comforting Christianity, gentle Jesus meek and mild, is a relatively modern development; for Milton, God's ways have to be *justified* to man, and the task is not an easy one.

In the final scene we find Lear creating a play world, the reconciliation with Cordelia allowing nothing more than a childish fantasy:

> Come, let's away to prison.
> We two alone will sing like birds i' th' cage.
> (V.3.8–9)

The point about birds in a cage is that they are happier than we are. Lear conceives of themselves getting clear out of the world of action and passion, spies for a God who has left the world unattended (why else would God need spies?), and thus creating the only permanence in a world of change. Of course this is a fantasy, not merely because of the real pathos of Lear's condition, but because it leaves out of account all the other realities of his world – the villainy of Edmund, who has ordered them killed; but also the realities of what even the men of good will in this play are like. Albany has to be *reminded* by Kent of the king and Cordelia, and he replies, "Great thing of us forgot!" (V.3.212). Forgetting a great thing makes it a nothing. Cordelia and Lear are killed as much by passive forgetfulness as by active villainy. Even in the play's last moments, lack of awareness is the destructive element.

Albany's pious prayer, "The gods defend her" (233), is immediately followed by Lear carrying Cordelia's corpse, howling like a beast; and it seems to Kent and Edgar the Day of Judgment –"Is this the promised end?" "Or image of that horror?" (240–41) – though characteristically it seems real to Kent, an image to Edgar. For Lear now, the only possible redemption is that Cordelia might not be dead. For a moment he thinks that she is alive, cruelly deceived; and then, when it is clear that she is not, raging again, he accuses the best and most faithful of friends, Kent and Edgar, of having murdered her. Goodwill counts for nothing, nothing redeems sorrows; Kent says it: "All's cheerless, dark, and deadly" (267). The final realization, the final truth of plain-speaking, is five *never*s:

> Thou'lt come no more.
> Never, never, never, never, never.
> (285–86)

Lear heartbreakingly extends Cordelia's *nothing* into the scheme of time. He returns momentarily to the fantasy that she lives –"Look on her! Look, her lips"– and with that false hope he dies.

It is important to emphasize that the exceptional bleakness of this conclusion is all Shakespeare's. In the story as he found it in every one of the sources, Cordelia's army is victorious, and Lear reascends his throne. Kent's simple eulogy does no more than accept the facts, and proposes no moral:

> He hates him
> That would upon the rack of this tough world
> Stretch him out longer.

The world is an instrument of torture, and the only comfort is in the nothing, the never, of death. The heroic vision is of suffering, unredeemed and unmitigated. Kent says, "The wonder is, he hath endured so long."

STEPHEN ORGEL
Stanford University

Note on the Text

King Lear has come down to us in two significantly different versions, a quarto published in 1608 and the text printed in the First Folio of 1623. Each of these includes material missing from the other: the folio has 115 lines not in the quarto, while the quarto has 285 lines (including a whole scene, and a large part of another) not in the folio. There are many smaller variations as well, in individual words, speech designations, lineation. It is generally, though not universally, agreed now that the quarto represents a version of the heavily corrected and revised manuscript that came from Shakespeare's hand, and that the folio represents a later performing version of the play. The implication is that the quarto represents the play *before* it was performed, the play as it went to the acting company to be transcribed and turned into a performing text, and that the folio version represents the performing text, though not necessarily the only version the company had performed in the years between 1605 and 1623.

Since Lewis Theobald's edition of Shakespeare's plays, published in 1733, the standard text of *King Lear* has been a conflation of the quarto and folio texts, with the presumption being that both are cut versions of a longer original. Because the two texts disagree on many matters, however, it is not possible simply to combine them, and a good deal of editorial judgment has always been required to produce a final version. Even editors who do not believe that behind the two texts lies a single Shakespearean original have nevertheless, until recently, preferred a conflated text simply because it gives us more Shakespeare – the quarto, indeed, is our only source for one of the most famous moments in the play, Lear's mock-trial of his daughters in III.6, and even if we believe Shakespeare edited this out of the final script, it is a scene later actors, directors, and editors have been loath to lose.

The play as presented in this volume is the traditional conflated text. It is substantially that prepared by Alfred Harbage for the old Pelican series, which in turn derives ultimately from the eighteenth-century text established by Theobald. (New glosses and notes have been provided.) Passages found only in the quarto are enclosed in roman brackets. For readers who wish to read the play in its two separate states, a companion volume in this series includes a two-text *King Lear*, with a discussion of the differences, and full textual notes.

King Lear

[Names of the Actors

LEAR, *King of Britain*
KING OF FRANCE
GONERIL, *Lear's eldest daughter*
DUKE OF ALBANY, *Goneril's husband*
REGAN, *Lear's second daughter*
DUKE OF CORNWALL, *Regan's husband*
CORDELIA, *Lear's youngest daughter*
DUKE OF BURGUNDY
EARL OF KENT
EARL OF GLOUCESTER
EDGAR, *Gloucester's elder son, later disguised as Tom o' Bedlam*
EDMUND, *Gloucester's younger, bastard son*
OSWALD, *Goneril's steward*
OLD MAN, *Gloucester's tenant*
CURAN, *Gloucester's servant*
FOOL, *attending on Lear*
DOCTOR
SERVANTS, CAPTAINS, HERALD, KNIGHTS, MESSENGERS, GENTLEMEN, SOLDIERS, *etc.*

Scene: *Britain*]

*

King Lear

I.1 *Enter Kent, Gloucester, and Edmund.*

KENT I thought the king had more affected the Duke of Albany than Cornwall.

GLOUCESTER It did always seem so to us, but now in the division of the kingdom, it appears not which of the dukes he values most, for qualities are so weighed that curiosity in neither can make choice of either's moiety.

KENT Is not this your son, my lord?

GLOUCESTER His breeding, sir, hath been at my charge. I have so often blushed to acknowledge him that now I am brazed to't.

KENT I cannot conceive you.

GLOUCESTER Sir, this young fellow's mother could, whereupon she grew round-wombed and had indeed, sir, a son for her cradle ere she had a husband for her bed. Do you smell a fault?

KENT I cannot wish the fault undone, the issue of it being so proper.

GLOUCESTER But I have a son, sir, by order of law, some year elder than this, who yet is no dearer in my account: though this knave came something saucily to the world before he was sent for, yet was his mother fair; there was

---

I.1 Lear's palace **s.d.** *Gloucester* (pronounced "Gloster") **1–2** *more affected . . . than* preferred . . . to **2** *Albany* i.e., Scotland **5** *equalities . . . weighed* their qualities are so equal **6** *curiosity . . . moiety* thorough examination cannot find either's share preferable **10** *brazed* brazened **11** *conceive* understand **17** *proper* handsome **18** *by . . . law* legitimate **19** *account* esteem **20** *something saucily* somewhat impertinently

22 good sport at his making, and the whoreson must be acknowledged. Do you know this noble gentleman, Edmund?

EDMUND No, my lord.

GLOUCESTER My Lord of Kent. Remember him hereafter as my honorable friend.

EDMUND My services to your lordship.

29 KENT I must love you, and sue to know you better.

30 EDMUND Sir, I shall study deserving.

31 GLOUCESTER He hath been out nine years, and away he
32 shall again.

[Sound a] Sennet.

The king is coming.

Enter [one bearing a coronet, then] King Lear, [then the Dukes of] Cornwall, [and] Albany, [next] Goneril, Regan, Cordelia, and Attendants.

LEAR

Attend the lords of France and Burgundy, Gloucester.

GLOUCESTER

I shall, my lord. *Exit [with Edmund].*

LEAR

36 Meantime we shall express our darker purpose.
Give me the map there. Know that we have divided
38 In three our kingdom; and 'tis our fast intent
To shake all cares and business from our age,
40 Conferring them on younger strengths while we
41 Unburdened crawl toward death. Our son of Cornwall,
And you our no less loving son of Albany,
43 We have this hour a constant will to publish
44 Our daughters' several dowers, that future strife
May be prevented now. The princes, France and Burgundy,

---

22 *whoreson* (literally "bastard," but the word was also an affectionate term, like "scamp") **29** *sue* seek **30** *study deserving* undertake to deserve it **31** *out* away **32 s.d.** *sennet* trumpet fanfare **36** *darker purpose* secret plan **38** *fast intent* firm intention **41** *son* son-in-law **43** *constant . . . publish* determination to express publicly **44** *several dowers* individual dowries

Great rivals in our youngest daughter's love,
Long in our court have made their amorous sojourn,
And here are to be answered. Tell me, my daughters
(Since now we will divest us both of rule,
Interest of territory, cares of state), 50
Which of you shall we say doth love us most,
That we our largest bounty may extend
Where nature doth with merit challenge. Goneril, 53
Our eldest born, speak first.

GONERIL

Sir, I love you more than word can wield the matter; 55
Dearer than eyesight, space, and liberty; 56
Beyond what can be valuèd, rich or rare;
No less than life, with grace, health, beauty, honor;
As much as child e'er loved, or father found;
A love that makes breath poor, and speech unable. 60
Beyond all manner of so much I love you.

CORDELIA *[Aside]*

What shall Cordelia speak? Love, and be silent.

LEAR

Of all these bounds, even from this line to this,
With shadowy forests and with champaigns riched, 64
With plenteous rivers and wide-skirted meads, 65
We make thee lady. To thine and Albany's issues 66
Be this perpetual. – What says our second daughter,
Our dearest Regan, wife of Cornwall?

REGAN

I am made of that self mettle as my sister, 69
And prize me at her worth. In my true heart 70
I find she names my very deed of love;
Only she comes too short, that I profess 72
Myself an enemy to all other joys

---

50 *Interest of* legal title to **53** *nature . . . challenge* the claims of natural affection are as strong as those of merit **55** *wield the matter* express the subject **56** *space* scope (to enjoy "liberty") **60** *breath* voice **64** *shadowy* shady; *champaigns riched* cultivated plains **65** *wide-skirted meads* spreading meadows **66** *issues* heirs **69** *self* same **70** *prize me* value myself **72** *that* in that

74 Which the most precious square of sense possesses,
75 And find I am alone felicitate
In your dear highness' love.
CORDELIA *[Aside]* Then poor Cordelia;
And yet not so, since I am sure my love's
More ponderous than my tongue.
LEAR
To thee and thine hereditary ever
80 Remain this ample third of our fair kingdom,
81 No less in space, validity, and pleasure
Than that conferred on Goneril. – Now, our joy,
83 Although our last and least, to whose young love
The vines of France and milk of Burgundy
85 Strive to be interessed, what can you say to draw
A third more opulent than your sisters? Speak.
CORDELIA Nothing, my lord.
LEAR Nothing?
CORDELIA Nothing.
LEAR
90 Nothing will come of nothing. Speak again.
CORDELIA
Unhappy that I am, I cannot heave
My heart into my mouth. I love your majesty
93 According to my bond, no more nor less.
LEAR
How, how, Cordelia? Mend your speech a little,
Lest you may mar your fortunes.
CORDELIA Good my lord,
96 You have begot me, bred me, loved me. I
Return those duties back as are right fit,
Obey you, love you, and most honor you.
Why have my sisters husbands if they say

---

74 *most . . . possesses* measure of perception holds to be most precious (?) **75** *felicitate* made happy **81** *validity* value **83** *least* smallest **85** *interessed* entitled to a share **90** *Nothing . . . nothing* (quoting a famous scholastic maxim derived from Aristotle, *nihil ex nihilo fit*) **93** *bond* duty **96–97** *I . . . fit* I am properly dutiful in return

They love you all? Haply, when I shall wed, *100*
That lord whose hand must take my plight shall carry 101
Half my love with him, half my care and duty.
Sure I shall never marry like my sisters,
[To love my father all.]

LEAR But goes thy heart with this?

CORDELIA Ay, my good lord.

LEAR So young, and so untender?

CORDELIA So young, my lord, and true. 108

LEAR

Let it be so, thy truth then be thy dower!
For, by the sacred radiance of the sun, *110*
The mysteries of Hecate and the night, 111
By all the operation of the orbs 112
From whom we do exist and cease to be,
Here I disclaim all my paternal care,
Propinquity, and property of blood, 115
And as a stranger to my heart and me
Hold thee from this forever. The barbarous Scythian, 117
Or he that makes his generation messes 118
To gorge his appetite, shall to my bosom
Be as well neighbored, pitied, and relieved, *120*
As thou my sometime daughter.

KENT Good my liege –

LEAR

Peace, Kent!
Come not between the dragon and his wrath.
I loved her most, and thought to set my rest
On her kind nursery. – Hence and avoid my sight! – 125
So be my grave my peace as here I give 126
Her father's heart from her! Call France – who stirs?

---

101 *plight* marriage vow **108** *true* honest **111** *Hecate* goddess of the underworld and patron of witchcraft **112** *operation . . . orbs* astrological influences **115** *Propinquity . . . blood* blood relationship **117** *this* this time; *Scythian* Crimean tribesman, notorious for cruelty **118** *makes . . . messes* devours his children **125** *nursery* care **126** *So . . . peace* let my only peace be in my grave

Call Burgundy. Cornwall and Albany,
With my two daughters' dowers digest the third;
130 Let pride, which she calls plainness, marry her.
I do invest you jointly with my power,
132 Preeminence, and all the large effects
133 That troop with majesty. Ourself, by monthly course,
134 With reservation of an hundred knights,
By you to be sustained, shall our abode
Make with you by due turn. Only we shall retain
137 The name, and all th' addition to a king. The sway,
Revenue, execution of the rest,
Belovèd sons, be yours; which to confirm,
140 This coronet part between you.

KENT Royal Lear,
Whom I have ever honored as my king,
Loved as my father, as my master followed,
As my great patron thought on in my prayers –

LEAR
144 The bow is bent and drawn; make from the shaft.

KENT
145 Let it fall rather, though the fork invade
The region of my heart. Be Kent unmannerly
When Lear is mad. What wouldst thou do, old man?
Think'st thou that duty shall have dread to speak
149 When power to flattery bows? To plainness honor's bound
150 When majesty falls to folly. Reserve thy state,
And in thy best consideration check
152 This hideous rashness. Answer my life my judgment,
Thy youngest daughter does not love thee least,

---

132 *large effects* rich trappings **133** *troop with* accompany; *by . . . course* month by month **134** *With reservation of* legally retaining **137** *all th' addition* i.e., the honors and prerogatives; *sway* authority **140** *coronet* (which would have crowned Cordelia) **144** *make from* get out of the way of **145** *fall* strike; *fork* (two-pronged) arrowhead **149** *plainness* straight talk **150** *Reserve . . . state* retain your authority **152** *Answer my life* I stake my life on

Nor are those empty-hearted whose low sounds
Reverb no hollowness.

LEAR Kent, on thy life, no more!

KENT
My life I never held but as a pawn
To wage against thine enemies; ne'er fear to lose it,
Thy safety being motive.

LEAR Out of my sight!

KENT
See better, Lear, and let me still remain
The true blank of thine eye.

LEAR Now by Apollo –

KENT
Now by Apollo, king,
Thou swear'st thy gods in vain.

LEAR O vassal! Miscreant! *[Grasping his sword]*

ALBANY, CORNWALL Dear sir, forbear!

KENT
Kill thy physician, and thy fee bestow
Upon the foul disease. Revoke thy gift,
Or, whilst I can vent clamor from my throat,
I'll tell thee thou dost evil.

LEAR Hear me, recreant,
On thine allegiance, hear me!
That thou hast sought to make us break our vows,
Which we durst never yet, and with strained pride
To come betwixt our sentence and our power,
Which nor our nature nor our place can bear,
Our potency made good, take thy reward.

---

155 *Reverb no hollowness* do not resonate hollowly 157 *pawn* both stake and the least valuable chess piece 158 *wage* wager, risk 159 *motive* motivation 161 *still* always 162 *true blank* exact bull's-eye 163 *Apollo* the sun god 166 *Miscreant* both villain and infidel 167 *Cornwall* (or Cordelia: F's speech heading is *Cor.*) 171 *recreant* traitor 173 *That* since 174 *strained* excessive 175 *our power* the power to execute it 176 *place* royal office 177 *Our . . . good* hereby demonstrating my power

Five days we do allot thee for provision
To shield thee from disasters of the world,
180 And on the sixth to turn thy hated back
Upon our kingdom. If, on the tenth day following,
182 Thy banished trunk be found in our dominions,
The moment is thy death. Away! By Jupiter,
This shall not be revoked.

KENT

185 Fare thee well, king. Sith thus thou wilt appear,
Freedom lives hence, and banishment is here.
[To Cordelia]
The gods to their dear shelter take thee, maid,
That justly think'st and hast most rightly said.
[To Regan and Goneril]
189 And your large speeches may your deeds approve,
190 That good effects may spring from words of love.
Thus Kent, O princes, bids you all adieu;
192 He'll shape his old course in a country new. *Exit.*

Flourish. Enter Gloucester, with France and Burgundy, Attendants.

GLOUCESTER

Here's France and Burgundy, my noble lord.

LEAR

My Lord of Burgundy,
We first address toward you, who with this king
Hath rivaled for our daughter. What in the least
Will you require in present dower with her,
Or cease your quest of love?

BURGUNDY Most royal majesty,
I crave no more than hath your highness offered,
200 Nor will you tender less.

LEAR Right noble Burgundy,
When she was dear to us, we did hold her so;

---

182 *trunk* body **185** *Sith* since **189** *your . . . approve* i.e., may your actions justify your words **192 s.d.** *Flourish* fanfare **200** *tender* offer

But now her price is fallen. Sir, there she stands.
If aught within that little seeming substance, 203
Or all of it, with our displeasure pieced 204
And nothing more, may fitly like your grace, 205
She's there, and she is yours.

BURGUNDY I know no answer.

LEAR
Will you, with those infirmities she owes, 207
Unfriended, new-adopted to our hate,
Dowered with our curse, and strangered with our oath, 209
Take her or leave her? *210*

BURGUNDY Pardon me, royal sir;
Election makes not up on such conditions. 211

LEAR
Then leave her, sir, for by the power that made me
I tell you all her wealth. *[To France]* For you, great king,
I would not from your love make such a stray 214
To match you where I hate; therefore beseech you
T' avert your liking a more worthier way 216
Than on a wretch whom Nature is ashamed
Almost t' acknowledge hers.

FRANCE This is most strange,
That she whom even but now was your best object,
The argument of your praise, balm of your age, 220
The best, the dearest, should in this trice of time
Commit a thing so monstrous to dismantle 222
So many folds of favor. Sure her offense
Must be of such unnatural degree
That monsters it, or your fore-vouched affection 225

---

203 *aught* anything; *little . . . substance* both mere shell of a person and person with few pretensions **204** *pieced* joined **205** *like* please **207** *owes* owns **209** *strangered with* made a stranger by **211** *Election . . . conditions* choice is impossible on such terms **214** *make . . . stray* stray so far as **216** *avert* turn **220** *argument* theme **222** *to dismantle* as to strip off **225** *monsters it* makes it monstrous **225–26** *your . . . taint* the love you previously swore must now appear suspect

Fall into taint; which to believe of her
Must be a faith that reason without miracle
Should never plant in me.

CORDELIA *[To Lear]* I yet beseech your majesty,
229 If for I want that glib and oily art
230 To speak and purpose not, since what I well intend
I'll do't before I speak, that you make known
It is no vicious blot, murder, or foulness,
No unchaste action or dishonored step
That hath deprived me of your grace and favor;
But even for want of that for which I am richer –
236 A still-soliciting eye, and such a tongue
That I am glad I have not, though not to have it
Hath lost me in your liking.

LEAR Better thou
Hadst not been born than not t' have pleased me better.

FRANCE
240 Is it but this? A tardiness in nature
Which often leaves the history unspoke
That it intends to do. My Lord of Burgundy,
What say you to the lady? Love's not love
244 When it is mingled with regards that stands
Aloof from th' entire point. Will you have her?
She is herself a dowry.

BURGUNDY Royal king,
Give but that portion which yourself proposed,
And here I take Cordelia by the hand,
Duchess of Burgundy.

LEAR
250 Nothing. I have sworn. I am firm.

BURGUNDY
I am sorry then you have so lost a father
That you must lose a husband.

---

229 *for I want* because I lack **236** *still-soliciting* always begging **244–45** *regards . . . point* considerations irrelevant to love

CORDELIA
Peace be with Burgundy.
Since that respects of fortune are his love, 254
I shall not be his wife.

FRANCE
Fairest Cordelia, that art most rich being poor,
Most choice forsaken, and most loved despised,
Thee and thy virtues here I seize upon.
Be it lawful I take up what's cast away.
Gods, gods! 'Tis strange that from their cold'st neglect *260*
My love should kindle to inflamed respect. 261
Thy dowerless daughter, king, thrown to my chance,
Is queen of us, of ours, and our fair France.
Not all the dukes of wat'rish Burgundy 264
Can buy this unprized precious maid of me. 265
Bid them farewell, Cordelia, though unkind.
Thou losest here, a better where to find. 267

LEAR
Thou hast her, France; let her be thine, for we
Have no such daughter, nor shall ever see
That face of hers again. Therefore be gone, *270*
Without our grace, our love, our benison. 271
Come, noble Burgundy.
Flourish. Exeunt [Lear, Burgundy, Cornwall, Albany, Gloucester, and Attendants].

FRANCE *[To Cordelia]*
Bid farewell to your sisters.

CORDELIA
The jewels of our father, with washed eyes 274
Cordelia leaves you. I know you what you are;
And, like a sister, am most loath to call
Your faults as they are named. Love well our father. 277

---

254 *respects . . . fortune* considerations of wealth **261** *inflamed respect* ardent admiration **264** *wat'rish* (1) well irrigated, (2) weak, wishy-washy **265** *unprized* unappreciated **267** *where* elsewhere **271** *benison* blessing **274** *washed* tearful **277** *as . . . named* by their real names

To your professèd bosoms I commit him;
But yet, alas, stood I within his grace,
I would prefer him to a better place.
So farewell to you both.

REGAN
Prescribe not us our duty.

GONERIL Let your study
Be to content your lord, who hath received you
At fortune's alms. You have obedience scanted,
And well are worth the want that you have wanted.

CORDELIA
Time shall unfold what plighted cunning hides,
Who covers faults, at last with shame derides.
Well may you prosper.

FRANCE Come, my fair Cordelia.
Exeunt France and Cordelia.

GONERIL Sister, it is not little I have to say of what most nearly appertains to us both. I think our father will hence tonight.

REGAN That's most certain, and with you; next month with us.

GONERIL You see how full of changes his age is. The observation we have made of it hath not been little. He always loved our sister most and with what poor judgment he hath now cast her off appears too grossly.

REGAN 'Tis the infirmity of his age; yet he hath ever but slenderly known himself.

GONERIL The best and soundest of his time hath been but rash; then must we look from his age to receive not alone the imperfections of long-engraffed condition,

---

278 *professèd bosoms* proclaimed love **280** *prefer* promote **284** *At . . . alms* as charity from fortune **285** *well . . . wanted* are properly deprived of what you yourself have lacked **287** *Who . . . derides* i.e., time finally exposes hidden faults to shame **297** *grossly* obviously **300** *The . . . been* even at his best he was **301** *then* therefore **302** *long-engraffed* deep-seated

but therewithal the unruly waywardness that infirm 303
and choleric years bring with them.

REGAN Such unconstant starts are we like to have from 305
him as this of Kent's banishment.

GONERIL There is further compliment of leave-taking 307
between France and him. Pray you let us hit together; if 308
our father carry authority with such disposition as he
bears, this last surrender of his will but offend us. 310

REGAN We shall further think of it.

GONERIL We must do something, and i' th' heat. 312

Exeunt.

*

❧ **I.2** *Enter Bastard [Edmund, solus, with a letter].*

EDMUND

Thou, Nature, art my goddess; to thy law
My services are bound. Wherefore should I
Stand in the plague of custom, and permit 3
The curiosity of nations to deprive me, 4
For that I am some twelve or fourteen moonshines 5
Lag of a brother? Why bastard? Wherefore base, 6
When my dimensions are as well compact, 7
My mind as generous, and my shape as true, 8
As honest madam's issue? Why brand they us 9
With base? with baseness? Bastardy base? Base? 10
Who, in the lusty stealth of nature, take 11
More composition and fierce quality 12

---

303 *therewithal* along with that **305** *unconstant starts* fits of impulsiveness **307** *compliment* formality **308** *hit* consult **310** *last surrender* recent abdication **312** *i' th' heat* immediately ("while the iron is hot")

I.2 Gloucester's house **3** *Stand . . . custom* submit to the affliction of convention (whereby the eldest son inherits everything, and illegitimate sons have no claim on the estate) **4** *curiosity* (legal) technicalities **5** *For that* because; *moonshines* months **6** *Lag of* younger than **7** *compact* composed **8** *My . . . generous* I am as well supplied with intelligence **9** *honest* chaste (i.e., married) **11** *the . . . nature* natural lust practiced in secret **12** *composition* physical excellence; *fierce* vigorous

Than doth, within a dull, stale, tired bed,
14 Go to th' creating a whole tribe of fops
15 Got 'tween asleep and wake? Well then,
16 Legitimate Edgar, I must have your land.
Our father's love is to the bastard Edmund
As to th' legitimate. Fine word, "legitimate."
19 Well, my legitimate, if this letter speed,
20 And my invention thrive, Edmund the base
Shall top th' legitimate. I grow, I prosper.
Now, gods, stand up for bastards.

Enter Gloucester. [Edmund reads a letter.]

GLOUCESTER
23 Kent banished thus? and France in choler parted?
24 And the king gone tonight? prescribed his pow'r?
25 Confined to exhibition? All this done
26 Upon the gad? – Edmund, how now? What news?

EDMUND So please your lordship, none.

GLOUCESTER Why so earnestly seek you to put up that letter?

30 EDMUND I know no news, my lord.

GLOUCESTER What paper were you reading?

EDMUND Nothing, my lord.

33 GLOUCESTER No? What needed then that terrible dispatch of it into your pocket? The quality of nothing hath not such need to hide itself. Let's see. Come, if it be nothing, I shall not need spectacles.

EDMUND I beseech you, sir, pardon me. It is a letter from my brother that I have not all o'erread; and for so much as I have perused, I find it not fit for your o'er-
40 looking.

GLOUCESTER Give me the letter, sir.

---

14 *fops* fools, sissies 15 *Got* begotten 16 *land* i.e., inheritance 19 *speed* succeed 20 *invention* scheme 23 *in . . . parted* departed in anger 24 *tonight* i.e., last night; *prescribed . . . pow'r* told how much power he is to have 25 *Confined . . . exhibition* limited to an allowance 26 *Upon . . . gad* suddenly, impulsively 33 *terrible* frightened

EDMUND I shall offend, either to detain or give it. The contents, as in part I understand them, are to blame.

GLOUCESTER Let's see, let's see.

EDMUND I hope, for my brother's justification, he wrote this but as an essay or taste of my virtue.

GLOUCESTER *Reads.* "This policy and reverence of age makes the world bitter to the best of our times; keeps our fortunes from us till our oldness cannot relish them. I begin to find an idle and fond bondage in the oppression of aged tyranny, who sways, not as it hath power, but as it is suffered. Come to me, that of this I may speak more. If our father would sleep till I waked him, you should enjoy half his revenue forever, and live the beloved of your brother. Edgar."
Hum! Conspiracy? "Sleep till I waked him, you should enjoy half his revenue." My son Edgar! Had he a hand to write this? A heart and brain to breed it in? When came you to this? Who brought it?

EDMUND It was not brought me, my lord; there's the cunning of it. I found it thrown in at the casement of my closet.

GLOUCESTER You know the character to be your brother's?

EDMUND If the matter were good, my lord, I durst swear it were his; but in respect of that, I would fain think it were not.

GLOUCESTER It is his.

EDMUND It is his hand, my lord; but I hope his heart is not in the contents.

---

43 *to blame* blameworthy **46** *essay . . . taste* (both words mean *test*) **47** *policy . . . of* policy of reverence for **48** *to . . . times* in the prime of our lives **50** *idle . . . fond* worthless and foolish **52** *suffered* allowed to do so **61–62** *casement . . . closet* window of my bedroom **63** *character* handwriting **65** *matter* substance **66** *in . . . that* i.e., considering the content; *fain* prefer to

GLOUCESTER Has he never before sounded you in this business?

EDMUND Never, my lord. But I have heard him oft maintain it to be fit that, sons at perfect age, and fathers declined, the father should be as ward to the son, and the son manage his revenue.

GLOUCESTER O villain, villain! His very opinion in the letter. Abhorred villain, unnatural, detested, brutish villain; worse than brutish! Go, sirrah, seek him. I'll apprehend him. Abominable villain! Where is he?

EDMUND I do not well know, my lord. If it shall please you to suspend your indignation against my brother till you can derive from him better testimony of his intent, you should run a certain course; where, if you violently proceed against him, mistaking his purpose, it would make a great gap in your own honor and shake in pieces the heart of his obedience. I dare pawn down my life for him that he hath writ this to feel my affection to your honor, and to no other pretense of danger.

GLOUCESTER Think you so?

EDMUND If your honor judge it meet, I will place you where you shall hear us confer of this and by an auricular assurance have your satisfaction, and that without any further delay than this very evening.

GLOUCESTER He cannot be such a monster.

[EDMUND Nor is not, sure.

GLOUCESTER To his father, that so tenderly and entirely loves him. Heaven and earth!] Edmund, seek him out; wind me into him, I pray you; frame the business after

---

71 *sounded you* sounded you out **74** *sons . . . age* when sons are mature **75** *as . . . to* placed under the guardianship of **79** *sirrah* (term of address used to a child or social inferior) **84** *run . . . course* be sure of your course of action; *where* whereas **87** *pawn down* stake **88** *feel* test **89** *pretense of danger* intent to do harm **91** *meet* appropriate **92–93** *an . . . assurance* the testimony of your own ears **99** *wind . . . him* worm your way into his confidence for me; *frame* arrange

your own wisdom. I would unstate myself to be in a 100
due resolution.

EDMUND I will seek him, sir, presently; convey the busi- 102
ness as I shall find means, and acquaint you withal. 103

GLOUCESTER These late eclipses in the sun and moon 104
portend no good to us. Though the wisdom of nature 105
can reason it thus and thus, yet nature finds itself 106
scourged by the sequent effects. Love cools, friendship
falls off, brothers divide. In cities, mutinies; in coun- 108
tries, discord; in palaces, treason; and the bond cracked
'twixt son and father. This villain of mine comes under *110*
the prediction, there's son against father; the king falls 111
from bias of nature, there's father against child. We 112
have seen the best of our time. Machinations,
hollowness, treachery, and all ruinous disorders follow 114
us disquietly to our graves. Find out this villain, Edmund; it shall lose thee nothing; do it carefully. And the noble and truehearted Kent banished; his offense, honesty. 'Tis strange. *Exit.*

EDMUND This is the excellent foppery of the world, that 119
when we are sick in fortune, often the surfeits of our own 120
behavior, we make guilty of our disasters the sun, the
moon, and stars; as if we were villains on necessity; fools
by heavenly compulsion; knaves, thieves, and treachers 123
by spherical predominance; drunkards, liars, and adul- 124
terers by an enforced obedience of planetary influence; 125
and all that we are evil in, by a divine thrusting on. An 126
admirable evasion of whoremaster man, to lay his goat- 127

100–1 *unstate . . . resolution* give up everything to resolve my doubts **102** *presently* immediately; *convey* conduct **103** *withal* with the result **104** *late* recent **105–6** *wisdom . . . thus* natural science can supply various explanations **106–7** *nature . . . effects* humanity (*nature*) suffers the consequences **108** *mutinies* rebellions **111** *prediction* ill omen **112** *bias of nature* his natural inclination **114** *hollowness* insincerity **119** *foppery* foolishness **120** *surfeits* overindulgences **123** *treachers* traitors **124** *spherical predominance* astrological influence **125** *of* to **126** *thrusting on* enforcement **127** *admirable* astonishing **127–28** *goatish* lecherous

ish disposition on the charge of a star. My father
129 compounded with my mother under the Dragon's tail,
130 and my nativity was under Ursa Major, so that it follows I am rough and lecherous. Fut! I should have been that I am, had the maidenliest star in the firmament twinkled on my bastardizing. Edgar –

Enter Edgar.

134 and pat he comes, like the catastrophe of the old com-
135 edy. My cue is villainous melancholy, with a sigh like
136 Tom o' Bedlam. – O, these eclipses do portend these
137 divisions. Fa, sol, la, mi.

EDGAR How now, brother Edmund; what serious contemplation are you in?

140 EDMUND I am thinking, brother, of a prediction I read this other day, what should follow these eclipses.

EDGAR Do you busy yourself with that?

143 EDMUND I promise you, the effects he writes of succeed unhappily: [as of unnaturalness between the child and the parent; death, dearth, dissolutions of ancient amities; divisions in state, menaces and maledictions against
147 king and nobles; needless diffidences, banishment of
148 friends, dissipation of cohorts, nuptial breaches, and I know not what.

150 EDGAR How long have you been a sectary astronomical?

EDMUND Come, come,] when saw you my father last?

EDGAR The night gone by.

EDMUND Spake you with him?

EDGAR Ay, two hours together.

---

129 *compounded* had sex **129–30** *Dragon's tail, Ursa Major* the constellations of Draco and the Great Bear **134–35** *catastrophe . . . comedy* conclusion in early comedy (i.e., often arbitrary or unmotivated, but at the appointed time) **135** *villainous* severe **136** *Tom o' Bedlam* a beggar from Bedlam (Bethlehem) Hospital, the London madhouse **137** *divisions* (1) conflicts, (2) musical phrases **143** *succeed* conclude **147** *diffidences* mistrust **148** *dissipation of cohorts* disbanding of armies **150** *sectary astronomical* astrological expert

EDMUND Parted you in good terms? Found you no displeasure in him by word nor countenance?

EDGAR None at all.

EDMUND Bethink yourself wherein you may have offended him; and at my entreaty forbear his presence until some little time hath qualified the heat of his displeasure, which at this instant so rageth in him that with the mischief of your person it would scarcely allay.

EDGAR Some villain hath done me wrong.

EDMUND That's my fear. I pray you have a continent forbearance till the speed of his rage goes slower; and, as I say, retire with me to my lodging, from whence I will fitly bring you to hear my lord speak. Pray ye, go; there's my key. If you do stir abroad, go armed.

EDGAR Armed, brother?

EDMUND Brother, I advise you to the best. Go armed. I am no honest man if there be any good meaning toward you. I have told you what I have seen and heard; but faintly, nothing like the image and horror of it. Pray you, away.

EDGAR Shall I hear from you anon?

EDMUND I do serve you in this business. *Exit [Edgar].*
A credulous father, and a brother noble,
Whose nature is so far from doing harms
That he suspects none; on whose foolish honesty
My practices ride easy. I see the business.
Let me, if not by birth, have lands by wit;
All with me's meet that I can fashion fit. *Exit.*

*

---

156 *countenance* look **160** *qualified* moderated **162** *the mischief of* injury to; *allay* be allayed **164** *continent* patient **167** *fitly* when it is appropriate **173–74** *the image . . . it* as horrible as it seemed **180** *practices* plots; *I . . . business* the plan is now clear **181** *wit* intelligence **182** *with . . . meet* suits me; *fashion fit* shape to serve my purpose

~ I.3 *Enter Goneril and Steward [Oswald].*

GONERIL
Did my father strike my gentleman for chiding of his fool?
OSWALD Ay, madam.
GONERIL
By day and night he wrongs me. Every hour
He flashes into one gross crime or other
That sets us all at odds. I'll not endure it.
His knights grow riotous, and himself upbraids us
On every trifle. When he returns from hunting,
I will not speak with him. Say I am sick.
If you come slack of former services,
You shall do well; the fault of it I'll answer.
[Horns within.]
OSWALD He's coming, madam; I hear him.
GONERIL
Put on what weary negligence you please,
You and your fellows. I'd have it come to question.
If he distaste it, let him to my sister,
Whose mind and mine I know in that are one,
[Not to be overruled. Idle old man,
That still would manage those authorities
That he hath given away. Now, by my life,
Old fools are babes again, and must be used
With checks as flatteries, when they are seen abused.]
Remember what I have said.
OSWALD Well, madam.
GONERIL
And let his knights have colder looks among you.
What grows of it, no matter; advise your fellows so.

I.3 Albany's castle **4** *crime* offense **9** *come . . . services* serve him less well than usual **10** *answer* answer for **13** *come . . . question* made an issue **14** *distaste* dislike **20** *checks . . . flatteries* rebukes as well as compliments; *they . . . seen* the compliments are

[I would breed from hence occasions, and I shall, 25
That I may speak.] I'll write straight to my sister 26
To hold my course. Prepare for dinner. *Exeunt.* 27

*

❧ I.4 *Enter Kent [disguised].*

KENT
If but as well I other accents borrow 1
That can my speech defuse, my good intent 2
May carry through itself to that full issue 3
For which I razed my likeness. Now, banished Kent, 4
If thou canst serve where thou dost stand condemned,
So may it come thy master whom thou lov'st 6
Shall find thee full of labors. 7
Horns within. Enter Lear, [Knight,] and Attendants.
LEAR Let me not stay a jot for dinner; go get it ready. 8
[Exit an Attendant.] How now, what art thou? 9
KENT A man, sir. 10
LEAR What dost thou profess? What wouldst thou with 11
us?
KENT I do profess to be no less than I seem, to serve him
truly that will put me in trust, to love him that is hon-
est, to converse with him that is wise and says little, to 15
fear judgment, to fight when I cannot choose, and to 16
eat no fish. 17
LEAR What art thou?

---

25 *breed . . . occasions* use this to provoke scenes **26** *speak* speak my mind **27** *hold . . . course* pursue the same course I do

I.4 **1** *If . . . borrow* i.e., if I disguise my voice as effectively as I do my appearance **2** *defuse* confuse, disguise **3** *issue* outcome **4** *razed . . . likeness* erased my appearance (including "razoring" his beard) **6** *come* happen that **7** *full . . . labors* i.e., hard at work; **s.d.** *Horns within* hunting horns offstage **8** *stay* wait **9** *what* who **11** *dost . . . profess* is your trade **15** *converse* associate **16** *fear judgment* show respect for authority; *choose* avoid it **17** *eat no fish* (a joke whose point has obviously been lost: not to be Catholic and thus forbidden to eat meat on Fridays? to be a meat eater only – i.e., manly?)

KENT A very honest-hearted fellow, and as poor as the
20 king.
LEAR If thou be'st as poor for a subject as he's for a king, thou art poor enough. What wouldst thou?
KENT Service.
LEAR Who wouldst thou serve?
KENT You.
LEAR Dost thou know me, fellow?
KENT No, sir, but you have that in your countenance
28 which I would fain call master.
LEAR What's that?
30 KENT Authority.
LEAR What services canst thou do?
32 KENT I can keep honest counsel, ride, run, mar a curious tale in telling it, and deliver a plain message bluntly. That which ordinary men are fit for I am qualified in, and the best of me is diligence.
LEAR How old art thou?
KENT Not so young, sir, to love a woman for singing, nor so old to dote on her for anything. I have years on my back forty-eight.
40 LEAR Follow me; thou shalt serve me. If I like thee no worse after dinner, I will not part from thee yet. Din-
42 ner, ho, dinner! Where's my knave? my fool? Go you and call my fool hither. *[Exit an Attendant.]*
Enter Steward [Oswald].
You, you, sirrah, where's my daughter?
OSWALD So please you –
Exit.
46 LEAR What says the fellow there? Call the clotpoll back. *[Exit Knight.]* Where's my fool? Ho, I think the world's asleep. *[Enter Knight.]* How now? Where's that mongrel?

---

28 *fain* like to **32** *keep . . . counsel* respect confidences **32–33** *curious* complicated **42** *knave* boy (the term could be affectionate) **46** *clotpoll* blockhead

KNIGHT He says, my lord, your daughter is not well. 50

LEAR Why came not the slave back to me when I called him?

KNIGHT Sir, he answered me in the roundest manner, he 53
would not.

LEAR He would not?

KNIGHT My lord, I know not what the matter is; but to
my judgment your highness is not entertained with 57
that ceremonious affection as you were wont. There's a 58
great abatement of kindness appears as well in the gen- 59
eral dependents, as in the duke himself also and your 60
daughter.

LEAR Ha? Sayst thou so?

KNIGHT I beseech you pardon me, my lord, if I be mistaken; for my duty cannot be silent when I think your highness wronged.

LEAR Thou but remember'st me of mine own conception. 66
I have perceived a most faint neglect of late,
which I have rather blamed as mine own jealous curios- 68
ity than as a very pretense and purpose of unkindness. I 69
will look further into't. But where's my fool? I have not 70
seen him this two days.

KNIGHT Since my young lady's going into France, sir, the fool hath much pined away.

LEAR No more of that; I have noted it well. Go you and tell my daughter I would speak with her. *[Exit Knight.]* Go you, call hither my fool. *[Exit an Attendant.]*

Enter Steward [Oswald].

O, you, sir, you! Come you hither, sir. Who am I, sir?

OSWALD My lady's father.

LEAR "My lady's father"? My lord's knave, you whoreson dog, you slave, you cur! 80

---

53 *roundest* rudest 57 *entertained* treated 58 *wont* accustomed to 59–60 *the . . . dependents* all the servants 66 *remember'st* remind 66–67 *conception* perception 68 *jealous curiosity* hypersensitiveness 69 *very pretense* real intention

OSWALD I am none of these, my lord; I beseech your pardon.

LEAR Do you bandy looks with me, you rascal?

[Strikes him.]

OSWALD I'll not be strucken, my lord.

85 KENT Nor tripped neither, you base football player.

[Trips up his heels.]

LEAR I thank thee, fellow. Thou serv'st me, and I'll love thee.

88 KENT Come, sir, arise, away. I'll teach you differences.
89 Away, away. If you will measure your lubber's length
90 again, tarry; but away. Go to! Have you wisdom? So.

[Pushes him out.]

LEAR Now, my friendly knave, I thank thee. There's
92 earnest of thy service.

[Gives money.] Enter Fool.

93 FOOL Let me hire him too. Here's my coxcomb.

[Offers Kent his cap.]

LEAR How now, my pretty knave? How dost thou?

FOOL Sirrah, you were best take my coxcomb.

KENT Why, fool?

FOOL Why? For taking one's part that's out of favor.
98 Nay, an thou canst not smile as the wind sits, thou'lt catch cold shortly. There, take my coxcomb. Why, this
100 fellow has banished two on's daughters, and did the third a blessing against his will. If thou follow him, thou must needs wear my coxcomb. – How now,
103 nuncle? Would I had two coxcombs and two daughters.

LEAR Why, my boy?

---

85 *football player* (football was a lower-class street game) **88** *differences* distinctions of rank **89** *measure . . . length* i.e., have me trip you up again; *lubber* oaf **92** *earnest of* a down payment on **93** *coxcomb* fool's cap **98** *an* if **98–99** *an . . . shortly* if you can't please those in power, you'll soon be out in the cold **100** *banished* as Kent says, "Freedom lives hence, and banishment is here" (I.1.186); *on's* of his **103** *nuncle* (mine) uncle

FOOL If I gave them all my living, I'd keep my coxcombs myself. There's mine; beg another of thy daughters. 105

LEAR Take heed, sirrah – the whip.

FOOL Truth's a dog must to kennel; he must be whipped out, when the Lady Brach may stand by th' fire and stink. 109

110

LEAR A pestilent gall to me. 111

FOOL Sirrah, I'll teach thee a speech.

LEAR Do.

FOOL Mark it, nuncle.

Have more than thou showest,
Speak less than thou knowest,
Lend less than thou owest, 117
Ride more than thou goest, 118
Learn more than thou trowest, 119
Set less than thou throwest; 120
Leave thy drink and thy whore,
And keep in-a-door,
And thou shalt have more
Than two tens to a score. 124

KENT This is nothing, fool.

FOOL Then 'tis like the breath of an unfeed lawyer – you gave me nothing for't. Can you make no use of nothing, nuncle? 126

LEAR Why, no, boy. Nothing can be made out of nothing.

130

FOOL *[To Kent]* Prithee tell him, so much the rent of his land comes to; he will not believe a fool. 131

---

105 *living* possessions **105–6** *I'd . . . myself* I'd be a double fool **109** *out* out of doors **109–10** *when . . . stink* brach = bitch; as Goneril and Regan are favored and the truthful Cordelia exiled **111** *gall* bitterness, sore **117** *owest* own **118** *goest* walk **119** *trowest* believe (i.e., don't believe everything you hear) **120** *Set . . . throwest* bet less than you win (at dice) **124** *score* twenty (i.e., you'll do better than break even) **126** *breath* speech; *unfeed* unpaid (lawyers proverbially will not plead without a fee) **131–32** *so . . . to* i.e., he no longer has any land, and therefore no income from it

LEAR A bitter fool.

FOOL Dost thou know the difference, my boy, between a bitter fool and a sweet one?

LEAR No, lad; teach me.

FOOL [That lord that counseled thee
To give away thy land,
Come place him here by me –
140 Do thou for him stand.
The sweet and bitter fool
142 Will presently appear;
143 The one in motley here,
The other found out there.

LEAR Dost thou call me fool, boy?

FOOL All thy other titles thou hast given away; that thou wast born with.

KENT This is not altogether fool, my lord.

149 FOOL No, faith; lords and great men will not let me. If I
150 had a monopoly out, they would have part on't. And ladies too, they will not let me have all the fool to myself; they'll be snatching.] Nuncle, give me an egg, and I'll give thee two crowns.

LEAR What two crowns shall they be?

FOOL Why, after I have cut the egg i' th' middle and eat
156 up the meat, the two crowns of the egg. When thou clovest thy crown i' th' middle and gav'st away both parts, thou bor'st thine ass on thy back o'er the dirt. Thou hadst little wit in thy bald crown when thou
160 gav'st thy golden one away. If I speak like myself in this,
161 let him be whipped that first finds it so.
162 *[Sings.]* Fools had ne'er less grace in a year,
163 For wise men are grown foppish,

---

142 *Will . . . appear* i.e., it will be immediately apparent which is which **143** *motley* the jester's particolored costume **149** *let me* i.e., let me have all the foolishness, be *altogether fool* **156** *two . . . egg* i.e., the empty shell **160** *like myself* i.e., like a fool **161** *that . . . so* i.e., for being a fool himself **162** *had . . . year* are now out of fashion **163** *foppish* foolish

And know not how their wits to wear, 164
Their manners are so apish. 165

LEAR When were you wont to be so full of songs, sirrah? 166

FOOL I have used it, nuncle, e'er since thou mad'st thy daughters thy mothers; for when thou gav'st them the rod, and put'st down thine own breeches,
[Sings.] Then they for sudden joy did weep, 170
And I for sorrow sung,
That such a king should play bopeep 172
And go the fools among.
Prithee, nuncle, keep a schoolmaster that can teach thy fool to lie. I would fain learn to lie. 175

LEAR An you lie, sirrah, we'll have you whipped. 176

FOOL I marvel what kin thou and thy daughters are. They'll have me whipped for speaking true; thou'lt have me whipped for lying; and sometimes I am whipped for holding my peace. I had rather be any 180 kind o' thing than a fool, and yet I would not be thee, nuncle; thou hast pared thy wit o' both sides and left nothing i' th' middle. Here comes one o' the parings.

Enter Goneril.

LEAR How now, daughter? What makes that frontlet on? 184 You are too much of late i' th' frown.

FOOL Thou wast a pretty fellow when thou hadst no need to care for her frowning. Now thou art an O without a figure. I am better than thou art now: I am a fool, 187 thou art nothing. *[To Goneril]* Yes, forsooth, I will hold my tongue. So your face bids me, though you say nothing. Mum, mum, 190

He that keeps nor crust nor crumb,
Weary of all, shall want some.

---

164 *their . . . wear* to use their heads **165** *apish* both stupid and imitative **166** *wont* accustomed **172** *play bopeep* i.e., act like a child **175** *fain* gladly **176** *An* if **184** *What . . . on* why are you wearing such a face (*frontlet* = forehead or a headband worn on it) **187–88** *an . . . figure* a zero with no number in front of it (i.e., nothing)

[Points at Lear.]
That's a shelled peasecod.

GONERIL
Not only, sir, this your all-licensed fool,
But other of your insolent retinue
Do hourly carp and quarrel, breaking forth
In rank and not-to-be-endurèd riots. Sir,
I had thought by making this well known unto you
To have found a safe redress, but now grow fearful,
By what yourself too late have spoke and done,
That you protect this course, and put it on
By your allowance; which if you should, the fault
Would not scape censure, nor the redresses sleep,
Which, in the tender of a wholesome weal,
Might in their working do you that offense,
Which else were shame, that then necessity
Will call discreet proceeding.

FOOL For you know, nuncle,
The hedge sparrow fed the cuckoo so long
That it's had it head bit off by it young.
So out went the candle, and we were left darkling.

LEAR Are you our daughter?

GONERIL
I would you would make use of your good wisdom
(Whereof I know you are fraught) and put away
These dispositions which of late transport you
From what you rightly are.

---

194 *shelled peasecod* empty pea pod **195** *all-licensed* allowed to do anything **198** *rank* gross **200** *safe redress* sure remedy **201** *too late* lately **202** *put . . . on* encourage it **204** *redresses sleep* punishment lie dormant **205** *tender . . . weal* government of a healthy commonwealth **206–8** *Might . . . proceeding* might humiliate you, but, being necessary, would be merely prudent; *necessity* = what the situation demands **210–11** *The . . . young* (the cuckoo lays its eggs in other birds' nests; the young cuckoos eventually destroy the sparrow that has been feeding them); *it . . . it* its . . . its **212** *darkling* in darkness **215** *fraught* full **216** *dispositions* moods

FOOL May not an ass know when the cart draws the
horse? Whoop, Jug, I love thee! 219

LEAR

Does any here know me? This is not Lear. *220*
Does Lear walk thus? speak thus? Where are his eyes?
Either his notion weakens, his discernings 222
Are lethargied – Ha! Waking? 'Tis not so. 223
Who is it that can tell me who I am?

FOOL Lear's shadow.

[LEAR

I would learn that; for, by the marks of sovereignty,
Knowledge, and reason, I should be false persuaded
I had daughters.

FOOL Which they will make an obedient father.]

LEAR Your name, fair gentlewoman? *230*

GONERIL

This admiration, sir, is much o' th' savor 231
Of other your new pranks. I do beseech you
To understand my purposes aright.
As you are old and reverend, should be wise.
Here do you keep a hundred knights and squires,
Men so disordered, so debauched and bold 236
That this our court, infected with their manners,
Shows like a riotous inn. Epicurism and lust 238
Makes it more like a tavern or a brothel
Than a graced palace. The shame itself doth speak 240
For instant remedy. Be then desired
By her that else will take the things she begs
A little to disquantity your train, 243
And the remainders that shall still depend 244

---

219 *Jug* Joan (generic name for a whore) **222** *notion* mind; *discernings* perceptions **223** *Waking* am I awake **231** *admiration* spectacle (something to be wondered at) **236** *bold* impudent **238** *Shows* looks; *Epicurism* gluttony **240** *graced* dignified **243** *disquantity . . . train* reduce the size of your retinue **244** *depend* be your dependents

245 To be such men as may besort your age,
Which know themselves, and you.

LEAR Darkness and devils!

247 Saddle my horses; call my train together.
Degenerate bastard, I'll not trouble thee:
Yet have I left a daughter.

GONERIL

250 You strike my people, and your disordered rabble
Make servants of their betters.

Enter Albany.

LEAR

Woe that too late repents. – [O, sir, are you come?]
Is it your will? Speak, sir. – Prepare my horses.
Ingratitude! thou marble-hearted fiend,
More hideous when thou show'st thee in a child
Than the sea monster.

ALBANY Pray, sir, be patient.

LEAR

258 Detested kite, thou liest.
259 My train are men of choice and rarest parts,
260 That all particulars of duty know
261 And in the most exact regard support
The worships of their name. O most small fault,
How ugly didst thou in Cordelia show!
264 Which, like an engine, wrenched my frame of nature
From the fixed place; drew from my heart all love
And added to the gall. O Lear, Lear, Lear!
267 Beat at this gate that let thy folly in

[Strikes his head.]

And thy dear judgment out. Go, go, my people.

---

245 *besort* befit **247** *Saddle . . . together* (Most editors send some knights off to do Lear's bidding, but it is more likely that everyone is immobilized with astonishment: he has to order the horses saddled again at line 253.) **258** *Detested kite* detestable bird of prey **259** *parts* qualities **261** *in . . . regard* with the most scrupulous attention **262** *worships* honor **264** *engine* machine **264–65** *my . . . place* the structure of my being from its foundations **267** *this gate* presumably his head

ALBANY
My lord, I am guiltless, as I am ignorant
Of what hath moved you. 270
LEAR It may be so, my lord.
Hear, Nature, hear; dear goddess, hear:
Suspend thy purpose if thou didst intend
To make this creature fruitful.
Into her womb convey sterility,
Dry up in her the organs of increase,
And from her derogate body never spring 276
A babe to honor her. If she must teem, 277
Create her child of spleen, that it may live 278
And be a thwart disnatured torment to her. 279
Let it stamp wrinkles in her brow of youth, 280
With cadent tears fret channels in her cheeks, 281
Turn all her mother's pains and benefits 282
To laughter and contempt, that she may feel
How sharper than a serpent's tooth it is
To have a thankless child. Away, away! *Exit.* 285
ALBANY
Now, gods that we adore, whereof comes this?
GONERIL
Never afflict yourself to know more of it,
But let his disposition have that scope 288
As dotage gives it.
Enter Lear.
LEAR
What, fifty of my followers at a clap? 290
Within a fortnight?
ALBANY What's the matter, sir?
LEAR
I'll tell thee. *[To Goneril]* Life and death, I am ashamed
That thou hast power to shake my manhood thus!

---

276 *derogate* debased **277** *teem* breed **278** *spleen* malice **279** *thwart disnatured* perverse, unnatural **281** *cadent* falling; *fret* wear **282** *pains* care **285 s.d.** (The fool apparently remains onstage.) **288** *disposition* mood

294 That these hot tears, which break from me perforce,
Should make thee worth them. Blasts and fogs upon thee!
296 Th' untented woundings of a father's curse
297 Pierce every sense about thee! Old fond eyes,
298 Beweep this cause again I'll pluck ye out
299 And cast you, with the waters that you loose,
300 To temper clay. [Yea, is it come to this?]
Ha! Let it be so. I have another daughter,
302 Who I am sure is kind and comfortable.
When she shall hear this of thee, with her nails
She'll flay thy wolvish visage. Thou shalt find
That I'll resume the shape which thou dost think
I have cast off forever.
Exit [Lear with Kent and Attendants].

GONERIL Do you mark that?

ALBANY
308 I cannot be so partial, Goneril,
To the great love I bear you –

GONERIL
310 Pray you, content. – What, Oswald, ho!
[To Fool]
You, sir, more knave than fool, after your master!

FOOL Nuncle Lear, nuncle Lear, tarry. Take the fool with thee.
A fox, when one has caught her,
And such a daughter,
316 Should sure to the slaughter,
317 If my cap would buy a halter.
So the fool follows after. *Exit.*

GONERIL
This man hath had good counsel – a hundred knights!

---

294 *perforce* i.e., against my will **296** *untented woundings* wounds too deep to be probed **297** *fond* foolish **298** *Beweep* if you weep over **299** *loose* let loose **300** *temper* soften **302** *comfortable* comforting **308–9** *partial . . . To* biased . . . by **316** *sure* surely be sent **317** *halter* noose

'Tis politic and safe to let him keep 320
At point a hundred knights – yes, that on every dream, 321
Each buzz, each fancy, each complaint, dislike, 322
He may enguard his dotage with their pow'rs 323
And hold our lives in mercy. – Oswald, I say! 324

ALBANY
Well, you may fear too far.

GONERIL
Safer than trust too far.
Let me still take away the harms I fear,
Not fear still to be taken. I know his heart.
What he hath uttered I have writ my sister.
If she sustain him and his hundred knights, *330*
When I have showed th' unfitness –
Enter Steward [Oswald]. How now, Oswald?
What, have you writ that letter to my sister?

OSWALD Ay, madam.

GONERIL
Take you some company, and away to horse.
Inform her full of my particular fear,
And thereto add such reasons of your own
As may compact it more. Get you gone, 337
And hasten your return. *[Exit Oswald.]* No, no, my lord,
This milky gentleness and course of yours, 339
Though I condemn not, yet under pardon, 340
You are much more a-tasked for want of wisdom 341
Than praised for harmful mildness.

ALBANY
How far your eyes may pierce I cannot tell;
Striving to better, oft we mar what's well.

GONERIL Nay then –

ALBANY Well, well; th' event. *Exeunt.* 346

*

---

320 *politic* prudent **321** *At point* armed **322** *buzz* murmur, whim **323** *enguard* safeguard **324** *in mercy* at his mercy **337** *compact* confirm **339** *milky . . . course* mild and gentle way **340** *under pardon* if you'll pardon me **341** *a-tasked* taken to task **346** *th' event* let's await the outcome

❧ I.5 *Enter Lear, Kent [disguised], and Fool.*

1 LEAR Go you before to Gloucester with these letters. Acquaint my daughter no further with anything you know
3 than comes from her demand out of the letter. If your diligence be not speedy, I shall be there afore you.

KENT I will not sleep, my lord, till I have delivered your letter. *Exit.*

FOOL If a man's brains were in's heels, were't not in dan-
8 ger of kibes?

LEAR Ay, boy.

10 FOOL Then I prithee be merry. Thy wit shall not go slipshod.

LEAR Ha, ha, ha.

13 FOOL Shalt see thy other daughter will use thee kindly;
14 for though she's as like this as a crab's like an apple, yet I can tell what I can tell.

LEAR What canst tell, boy?

FOOL She will taste as like this as a crab does to a crab.
18 Thou canst tell why one's nose stands i' th' middle on's face?

20 LEAR No.

FOOL Why, to keep one's eyes of either side's nose, that what a man cannot smell out he may spy into.

23 LEAR I did her wrong.

FOOL Canst tell how an oyster makes his shell?

LEAR No.

FOOL Nor I neither; but I can tell why a snail has a house.

I.5 **1** *before* ahead of me; *Gloucester* (apparently not the earl but the town, which would therefore be the location of Regan and Cornwall's castle); *these letters* this letter (i.e., the letters that comprise one message; cf. "these words") **3** *demand . . . of* questions prompted by **8** *kibes* chilblains **10–11** *shall . . . slipshod* will not have to wear slippers because of chilblains (the point is that feet with brains would not make this journey) **13** *Shalt* thou shalt; *kindly* both affectionately and after her kind – i.e., in the same way **14** *crab* crabapple, proverbially sour **18** *on's* of his **23** *her* Cordelia

LEAR Why?
FOOL Why, to put's head in; not to give it away to his daughters, and leave his horns without a case. 30
LEAR I will forget my nature. So kind a father! – Be my 31
horses ready?
FOOL Thy asses are gone about 'em. The reason why the 33
seven stars are no more than seven is a pretty reason.
LEAR Because they are not eight.
FOOL Yes indeed. Thou wouldst make a good fool.
LEAR To take't again perforce – Monster ingratitude! 37
FOOL If thou wert my fool, nuncle, I'd have thee beaten for being old before thy time.
LEAR How's that? *40*
FOOL Thou shouldst not have been old till thou hadst been wise.
LEAR
O, let me not be mad, not mad, sweet heaven!
Keep me in temper; I would not be mad! 44
[Enter a Gentleman.]
How now, are the horses ready?
GENTLEMAN Ready, my lord.
LEAR Come, boy.
FOOL
She that's a maid now, and laughs at my departure, 48
Shall not be a maid long, unless things be cut shorter.
Exeunt.

*

---

30 *horns* (with a quibble on the cuckold's horns, implying that Goneril and Regan are illegitimate) 31 *nature* paternal instincts 33–34 *the seven stars* the constellation the Pleiades 37 *To . . . perforce* to take it back forcibly (Lear either rages at Goneril's revocation of his privileges or contemplates reasserting his power) 44 *in temper* temperate, sane 48–49 *She . . . shorter* i.e., the maid who laughed at my leaving would be a fool and would not remain a virgin unless men were castrated

❧ **II.1** *Enter Bastard [Edmund] and Curan severally.*

EDMUND Save thee, Curan.
CURAN And you, sir. I have been with your father, and given him notice that the Duke of Cornwall and Regan his duchess will be here with him this night.
EDMUND How comes that?
CURAN Nay, I know not. You have heard of the news abroad – I mean the whispered ones, for they are yet but ear-kissing arguments?
EDMUND Not I. Pray you, what are they?
CURAN Have you heard of no likely wars toward, 'twixt the Dukes of Cornwall and Albany?
EDMUND Not a word.
CURAN You may do, then, in time. Fare you well, sir. *Exit.*

EDMUND
The duke be here tonight? The better best!
This weaves itself perforce into my business.
My father hath set guard to take my brother,
And I have one thing of a queasy question
Which I must act. Briefness and fortune, work!
– Brother, a word: descend. Brother, I say!
Enter Edgar.
My father watches. O sir, fly this place.
Intelligence is given where you are hid.
You have now the good advantage of the night.
Have you not spoken 'gainst the Duke of Cornwall?
He's coming hither; now i' th' night, i' th' haste,
And Regan with him. Have you nothing said

II.1 Gloucester's house **s.d.** *severally* separately **1** *Save thee* God save thee (a casual greeting like "good day") **8** *ear-kissing arguments* whispered matters **10** *toward* impending **14** *better best* very best **15** *perforce* necessarily **17** *queasy question* delicate problem **18** *Briefness . . . work* may speed and luck work for me **19** *descend* (possibly Edgar has appeared on the upper-stage gallery) **21** *Intelligence* information

Upon his party 'gainst the Duke of Albany? 26
Advise yourself. 27

EDGAR I am sure on't, not a word.

EDMUND

I hear my father coming. Pardon me:
In cunning I must draw my sword upon you.
Draw, seem to defend yourself; now quit you well. – 30
Yield! Come before my father! Light ho, here! –
Fly, brother. – Torches, torches! – So farewell.
Exit Edgar.
Some blood drawn on me would beget opinion 33
Of my more fierce endeavor.
[Cuts his arm.] I have seen drunkards
Do more than this in sport. – Father, father!
Stop, stop! No help?
Enter Gloucester, and Servants with torches.

GLOUCESTER

Now, Edmund, where's the villain?

EDMUND

Here stood he in the dark, his sharp sword out,
Mumbling of wicked charms, conjuring the moon
To stand auspicious mistress. 40

GLOUCESTER But where is he?

EDMUND

Look, sir, I bleed.

GLOUCESTER Where is the villain, Edmund?

EDMUND

Fled this way, sir, when by no means he could –

GLOUCESTER

Pursue him, ho! Go after. *[Exeunt some Servants.]*
By no means what?

EDMUND

Persuade me to the murder of your lordship;

---

26 *Upon . . . 'gainst* relating to his quarrel with **27** *Advise yourself* think about it; *on't* of it **30** *quit you* acquit yourself **33–34** *beget . . . endeavor* give the impression that I fought fiercely **40** *stand* act as his

But that I told him the revenging gods
'Gainst parricides did all the thunder bend;
Spoke with how manifold and strong a bond
The child was bound to th' father – sir, in fine,
Seeing how loathly opposite I stood
To his unnatural purpose, in fell motion
With his preparèd sword he charges home
My unprovided body, latched mine arm;
And when he saw my best alarumed spirits
Bold in the quarrel's right, roused to th' encounter,
Or whether ghasted by the noise I made,
Full suddenly he fled.

GLOUCESTER Let him fly far.
Not in this land shall he remain uncaught;
And found – dispatch. The noble duke my master,
My worthy arch and patron, comes tonight:
By his authority I will proclaim it
That he which finds him shall deserve our thanks,
Bringing the murderous coward to the stake;
He that conceals him, death.

EDMUND
When I dissuaded him from his intent
And found him pight to do it, with curst speech
I threatened to discover him. He replied,
"Thou unpossessing bastard, dost thou think,
If I would stand against thee, would the reposal
Of any trust, virtue, or worth in thee
Make thy words faithed? No. What I should deny

---

45 *But that* however 46 *thunder bend* thunderbolts aim 48 *in fine* finally 49 *loathly opposite* loathingly opposed 50 *fell motion* deadly action 51 *charges home* thrusts directly at 52 *unprovided* unprotected; *latched* hit 53 *best alarumed* fully aroused 54 *quarrel's right* justice of the cause 55 *ghasted* frightened 58 *found – dispatch* once found – death 59 *arch . . . patron* chief patron 65 *pight* determined; *curst* angry 66 *discover* expose 67 *unpossessing* unpropertied, landless 68 *reposal* placing 70 *faithed* believed; *What . . . should* whatever I would

(As this I would, ay, though thou didst produce
My very character) I'd turn it all 72
To thy suggestion, plot, and damnèd practice; 73
And thou must make a dullard of the world, 74
If they not thought the profits of my death
Were very pregnant and potential spirits 76
To make thee seek it." 77

GLOUCESTER O strange and fastened villain!
Would he deny his letter, said he? [I never got him.] 78
Tucket within.
Hark, the duke's trumpets. I know not why he comes.
All ports I'll bar; the villain shall not scape; 80
The duke must grant me that. Besides, his picture
I will send far and near, that all the kingdom
May have due note of him; and of my land,
Loyal and natural boy, I'll work the means
To make thee capable. 85
Enter Cornwall, Regan, and Attendants.

CORNWALL
How now, my noble friend? Since I came hither
(Which I can call but now) I have heard strange news. 87

REGAN
If it be true, all vengeance comes too short
Which can pursue th' offender. How dost, my lord?

GLOUCESTER
O madam, my old heart is cracked, it's cracked. 90

REGAN
What, did my father's godson seek your life?
He whom my father named, your Edgar?

GLOUCESTER
O lady, lady, shame would have it hid.

---

72 *character* handwriting – i.e., evidence in my own hand; *turn* ascribe **73** *practice* evil schemes **74** *make . . . world* consider everyone stupid **76** *pregnant . . . spirits* meaningful and powerful motives **77** *strange . . . fastened* unnatural and hardened **78** *got* fathered; **s.d.** *Tucket* trumpet signal **80** *ports* both seaports and town gates **85** *capable* legally able to inherit **87** *call but* say was only

REGAN
Was he not companion with the riotous knights
That tended upon my father?
GLOUCESTER
I know not, madam. 'Tis too bad, too bad.
EDMUND
Yes, madam, he was of that consort.
REGAN
98 No marvel then though he were ill affected.
99 'Tis they have put him on the old man's death,
100 To have th' expense and waste of his revenues.
I have this present evening from my sister
Been well informed of them, and with such cautions
That, if they come to sojourn at my house,
I'll not be there.
CORNWALL Nor I, assure thee, Regan.
Edmund, I hear that you have shown your father
A childlike office.
EDMUND It was my duty, sir.
GLOUCESTER
107 He did bewray his practice, and received
This hurt you see, striving to apprehend him.
CORNWALL
Is he pursued?
GLOUCESTER Ay, my good lord.
CORNWALL
110 If he be taken, he shall never more
111 Be feared of doing harm. Make your own purpose,
How in my strength you please. For you, Edmund,
Whose virtue and obedience doth this instant
So much commend itself, you shall be ours.
Natures of such deep trust we shall much need;
You we first seize on.

---

98 *though* that; *ill affected* disposed to evil 99 *put* set 100 *waste* plunder 107 *bewray . . . practice* expose Edgar's plot 111–12 *Make . . . please* carry out your intentions making what use you wish of my powers

EDMUND I shall serve you, sir,
Truly, however else. 117
GLOUCESTER For him I thank your grace.
CORNWALL
You know not why we came to visit you?
REGAN
Thus out of season, threading dark-eyed night. 120
Occasions, noble Gloucester, of some prize, 121
Wherein we must have use of your advice.
Our father he hath writ, so hath our sister,
Of differences, which I best thought it fit 124
To answer from our home. The several messengers 125
From hence attend dispatch. Our good old friend, 126
Lay comforts to your bosom, and bestow
Your needful counsel to our businesses, 128
Which craves the instant use. 129
GLOUCESTER I serve you, madam.
Your graces are right welcome. *Exeunt. Flourish.* 130

*

❧ **II.2** *Enter Kent [disguised] and Steward [Oswald], severally.*

OSWALD Good dawning to thee, friend. Art of this house? 1
KENT Ay. 2
OSWALD Where may we set our horses?
KENT I' th' mire.
OSWALD Prithee, if thou lov'st me, tell me. 5
KENT I love thee not.
OSWALD Why then, I care not for thee.

---

117 *however else* if nothing else **120** *out of season* untimely (i.e., traveling at night) **121** *prize* price, importance **124** *differences* quarrels **125** *answer . . . home* deal with away from home; *several* various **126** *attend* await **128** *needful* needed **129** *the . . . use* immediate action

II.2 **1** *Art of* are you a servant in **2** *Ay* (since the house is Gloucester's, Kent is lying, presumably as a way of picking a fight with Oswald) **5** *if . . . me* i.e., be kind enough to

KENT If I had thee in Lipsbury Pinfold, I would make thee care for me.

OSWALD Why dost thou use me thus? I know thee not.

KENT Fellow, I know thee.

OSWALD What dost thou know me for?

KENT A knave, a rascal, an eater of broken meats; a base, proud, shallow, beggarly, three-suited, hundred-pound, filthy worsted-stocking knave; a lily-livered, action-taking, whoreson, glass-gazing, superserviceable, finical rogue; one-trunk-inheriting slave; one that wouldst be a bawd in way of good service, and art nothing but the composition of a knave, beggar, coward, pander, and the son and heir of a mongrel bitch; one whom I will beat into clamorous whining if thou deny'st the least syllable of thy addition.

OSWALD Why, what a monstrous fellow art thou, thus to rail on one that is neither known of thee nor knows thee!

KENT What a brazen-faced varlet art thou to deny thou knowest me! Is it two days ago since I tripped up thy heels and beat thee before the king? *[Draws his sword.]* Draw, you rogue, for though it be night, yet the moon shines. I'll make a sop o' th' moonshine of you. You whoreson cullionly barbermonger, draw!

---

8 *Lipsbury Pinfold* the pen of my lips – i.e., between my teeth (jocularly, as a place name) **10** *use* treat **13** *broken meats* leftover food, fit for menials **14** *three-suited* (male household servants were furnished with three suits per year: Kent attacks Oswald's pretensions to gentility); *hundred-pound* the minimum annual income for a gentleman **15** *worsted-stocking* coarse wool stocking (a gentleman would wear silk); *lily-livered* cowardly; *action-taking* litigious (resorting to legal action instead of fighting) **16** *glass-gazing . . . finical* vain, toadying, fussy **17** *one-trunk-inheriting* owning no more than will fit in a single trunk **18** *a bawd . . . service* a pimp if asked **19** *composition* composite **22** *addition* title (i.e., the names I have just called you) **26** *varlet* rogue **30** *make . . . moonshine* fill you with holes so your body will sop up moonshine **31** *cullionly* despicable (cullions are testicles; the insult is analogous to calling someone a prick); *barbermonger* (a particularly inventive insult: on the model of whoremonger, a pimp for barbers, one who supplies them with clients, hence who caters to the needs of effeminate men)

OSWALD Away, I have nothing to do with thee.

KENT Draw, you rascal. You come with letters against the king, and take Vanity the puppet's part against the royalty of her father. Draw, you rogue, or I'll so carbonado your shanks. Draw, you rascal. Come your ways!

OSWALD Help, ho! Murder! Help!

KENT Strike, you slave! Stand, rogue! Stand, you neat slave! Strike!

[Beats him.]

OSWALD Help, ho! Murder, murder!

Enter Bastard [Edmund, with his rapier drawn], Cornwall, Regan, Gloucester, Servants.

EDMUND How now? What's the matter? Part!

KENT With you, goodman boy, if you please! Come, I'll flesh ye; come on, young master.

GLOUCESTER Weapons? Arms? What's the matter here?

CORNWALL Keep peace, upon your lives. He dies that strikes again. What is the matter?

REGAN The messengers from our sister and the king.

CORNWALL What is your difference? Speak.

OSWALD I am scarce in breath, my lord.

KENT No marvel, you have so bestirred your valor. You cowardly rascal, nature disclaims in thee. A tailor made thee.

CORNWALL Thou art a strange fellow. A tailor make a man?

KENT A tailor, sir. A stonecutter or a painter could not have made him so ill, though they had been but two years o' th' trade.

CORNWALL

Speak yet, how grew your quarrel?

---

34 *take . . . part* (support the vain, overdressed Goneril) **35** *carbonado* slash **36** *Come . . . ways* come on, get to it **38** *neat* prissy **42** *goodman boy* (both are deliberate insults to Edmund as a gentleman: *goodman* = yeoman or farmer) **43** *flesh ye* give you your first taste of blood **48** *difference* quarrel **51** *disclaims in* disowns **56** *ill* badly **57** *o' th'* at the

OSWALD This ancient ruffian, sir, whose life I have
60 spared at suit of his gray beard –
61 KENT Thou whoreson zed, thou unnecessary letter! My
62 lord, if you will give me leave, I will tread this unbolted
63 villain into mortar and daub the wall of a jakes with
64 him. Spare my gray beard, you wagtail?
CORNWALL
Peace, sirrah!
You beastly knave, know you no reverence?
KENT
Yes, sir, but anger hath a privilege.
CORNWALL
Why art thou angry?
KENT
That such a slave as this should wear a sword,
70 Who wears no honesty. Such smiling rogues as these
71 Like rats oft bite the holy cords a-twain
72 Which are too intrinse t' unloose; smooth every passion
73 That in the natures of their lords rebel,
Being oil to fire, snow to the colder moods;
75 Renege, affirm, and turn their halcyon beaks
76 With every gale and vary of their masters,
Knowing nought, like dogs, but following.
78 A plague upon your epileptic visage!
79 Smile you my speeches, as I were a fool?
80 Goose, if I had you upon Sarum Plain,
81 I'd drive ye cackling home to Camelot.

---

60 *at suit* at the plea **61** *zed* the letter *z* (*unnecessary* because its sound is also represented by *s*, and because it is not used in Latin) **62** *unbolted* unsifted (as flour or plaster) **63** *jakes* toilet **64** *wagtail* a bird that constantly wags its tail; hence a nervous or effeminate person **71** *holy cords* sacred bonds **72** *intrinse* intertwined; *smooth* flatter **73** *rebel* i.e., against reason **75** *Renege* deny; *halcyon* kingfisher; their beaks were said to be usable as weather vanes **76** *gale . . . vary* changing wind **78** *epileptic* grinning **79** *Smile you* do you smile at; *as* as if **80** *Sarum Plain* Salisbury Plain, near Winchester (Oswald is a goose because he is laughing, but it is not clear why Shakespeare associates geese with Salisbury Plain) **81** *Camelot* legendary capital of King Arthur, thought to have been on the site of Winchester

CORNWALL
What, art thou mad, old fellow?
GLOUCESTER
How fell you out? Say that.
KENT
No contraries hold more antipathy 84
Than I and such a knave.
CORNWALL
Why dost thou call him knave? What is his fault?
KENT
His countenance likes me not. 87
CORNWALL
No more perchance does mine, nor his, nor hers.
KENT
Sir, 'tis my occupation to be plain:
I have seen better faces in my time *90*
Than stands on any shoulder that I see
Before me at this instant.
CORNWALL This is some fellow
Who, having been praised for bluntness, doth affect 93
A saucy roughness, and constrains the garb 94
Quite from his nature. He cannot flatter, he;
An honest mind and plain – he must speak truth.
An they will take it, so; if not, he's plain. 97
These kind of knaves I know which in this plainness
Harbor more craft and more corrupter ends
Than twenty silly-ducking observants 100
That stretch their duties nicely. 101
KENT
Sir, in good faith, in sincere verity,
Under th' allowance of your great aspect,

---

84 *contraries* opposites **87** *His . . . not* I don't like his face **93** *affect* adopt **94–95** *constrains . . . nature* forces plain speaking away from its proper function (*garb* = style of speech; *his* = its) **97** *An* if; *so* well and good; *he's plain* his excuse is his bluntness **100** *silly . . . observants* bowing attendants **101** *nicely* excessively

Whose influence, like the wreath of radiant fire
105 On flick'ring Phoebus' front –
CORNWALL What mean'st by this?
106 KENT To go out of my dialect, which you discommend
107 so much. I know, sir, I am no flatterer. He that beguiled
you in a plain accent was a plain knave, which, for my
part, I will not be, though I should win your displea-
110 sure to entreat me to't.
CORNWALL *[To Oswald]* What was th' offense you
gave him?
OSWALD
I never gave him any.
113 It pleased the king his master very late
114 To strike at me, upon his misconstruction;
115 When he, compact, and flattering his displeasure,
Tripped me behind; being down, insulted, railed,
117 And put upon him such a deal of man
118 That worthied him, got praises of the king
119 For him attempting who was self-subdued;
120 And, in the fleshment of this dread exploit,
Drew on me here again.
KENT
122 None of these rogues and cowards
But Ajax is their fool.
CORNWALL Fetch forth the stocks!
You stubborn ancient knave, you reverent braggart,
We'll teach you.
KENT Sir, I am too old to learn.
Call not your stocks for me, I serve the king –
On whose employment I was sent to you;

---

105 *Phoebus' front* the sun god's forehead **106** *go . . . dialect* depart from my usual way of speaking **107–8** *He . . . you* whoever deceived you **110** *to . . . to't* i.e., even if you begged me to be a knave **113** *very late* recently **114** *misconstruction* misunderstanding me **115** *compact* in league with (the king) **117** *deal . . . man* macho act **118** *worthied him* made him a hero **119** *For . . . subdued* for attacking a man who refused to fight **120** *fleshment* excitement **122–23** *None . . . fool* (i.e., Oswald is making a fool out of Cornwall, whom Kent identifies with the dull-witted and boastful Greek hero Ajax)

You shall do small respect, show too bold malice
Against the grace and person of my master,
Stocking his messenger. *130*

CORNWALL
Fetch forth the stocks. As I have life and honor,
There shall he sit till noon.

REGAN
Till noon? Till night, my lord, and all night too.

KENT
Why, madam, if I were your father's dog,
You should not use me so.

REGAN Sir, being his knave, I will. 136

CORNWALL
This is a fellow of the selfsame color
Our sister speaks of. Come, bring away the stocks. 138
Stocks brought out.

GLOUCESTER
Let me beseech your grace not to do so.
[His fault is much, and the good king his master *140*
Will check him for't. Your purposed low correction
Is such as basest and contemnèd'st wretches
For pilf'rings and most common trespasses
Are punished with.]
The king his master needs must take it ill
That he, so slightly valued in his messenger,
Should have him thus restrained. 147

CORNWALL I'll answer that.

REGAN
My sister may receive it much more worse,
To have her gentleman abused, assaulted,
[For following her affairs. Put in his legs.] *150*
[Kent is put in the stocks.]

CORNWALL
Come, my lord, away!
Exit [with all but Gloucester and Kent].

---

136 *being* as you are 138 *away* forward 147 *answer* answer for

GLOUCESTER
I am sorry for thee, friend. 'Tis the duke's pleasure,
Whose disposition all the world well knows
154 Will not be rubbed nor stopped. I'll entreat for thee.

KENT
155 Pray do not, sir, I have watched and traveled hard.
Some time I shall sleep out, the rest I'll whistle.
157 A good man's fortune may grow out at heels.
Give you good morrow.

GLOUCESTER
The duke's to blame in this. 'Twill be ill taken. *Exit.*

KENT
160 Good king, that must approve the common saw,
161 Thou out of heaven's benediction com'st
To the warm sun.
163 Approach, thou beacon to this under globe,
164 That by thy comfortable beams I may
165 Peruse this letter. Nothing almost sees miracles
But misery. I know 'tis from Cordelia,
Who hath most fortunately been informed
168 Of my obscurèd course. And shall find time
From this enormous state, seeking to give
170 Losses their remedies. – All weary and o'erwatched,
171 Take vantage, heavy eyes, not to behold
This shameful lodging. Fortune, good night;
173 Smile once more; turn thy wheel.
[Sleeps.]

---

154 *rubbed* deflected (term from the game of bowls) **155** *watched* stayed awake **157** *grow . . . heels* wear thin **160** *approve . . . saw* prove the truth of the old saying **161–62** *Thou . . . sun* you go from God's blessing into the hot sun – i.e., you go from good to bad **163** *beacon* presumably the moon, since it is still night **164** *comfortable* comforting **165–66** *Nothing . . . misery* miracles are rarely seen by any but the miserable **168** *obscurèd* disguised **168–70** *And . . . remedies* (a famously incoherent crux: is Kent reading a bit of Cordelia's letter? [*enormous state* = terrible situation]) **170** *o'erwatched* too long without sleep **171** *Take vantage* take advantage (by falling asleep) **173** *turn . . . wheel* change my luck: the goddess Fortuna is depicted with a large vertical wheel, which she turns arbitrarily; Kent is now at the bottom

*

❧ II.3 *Enter Edgar.*

EDGAR

I heard myself proclaimed, 1
And by the happy hollow of a tree 2
Escaped the hunt. No port is free, no place
That guard and most unusual vigilance
Does not attend my taking. Whiles I may scape, 5
I will preserve myself; and am bethought 6
To take the basest and most poorest shape
That ever penury, in contempt of man, 8
Brought near to beast: my face I'll grime with filth,
Blanket my loins, elf all my hairs in knots, 10
And with presented nakedness outface 11
The winds and persecutions of the sky.
The country gives me proof and precedent 13
Of Bedlam beggars, who, with roaring voices, 14
Strike in their numbed and mortified bare arms 15
Pins, wooden pricks, nails, sprigs of rosemary;
And with this horrible object, from low farms, 17
Poor pelting villages, sheepcotes, and mills, 18
Sometimes with lunatic bans, sometime with prayers, 19
Enforce their charity. Poor Turlygod, poor Tom, 20
That's something yet: Edgar I nothing am. 21

Exit.

*

II.3 s.d. Kent remains onstage in the stocks, asleep, but he and Edgar are clearly not part of the same scene. **1** *proclaimed* i.e., as an outlaw **2** *happy hollow* i.e., lucky hiding place **5** *attend . . . taking* prepare to arrest me **6** *am bethought* have a plan **8** *of* for **10** *elf* tangle (into "elf locks") **11** *presented* the show of **13** *proof* experience **14** *Bedlam beggars* (see I.2.136) **15** *Strike* stick; *mortified* dead to pain **17** *object* spectacle **18** *pelting* paltry **19** *bans* curses **20** *Turlygod* (unexplained, but evidently another name for a Bedlam beggar) **21** *Edgar* i.e., as Edgar

❧ II.4 *Enter Lear, Fool, and Gentleman.*

LEAR
'Tis strange that they should so depart from home,
And not send back my messenger.
GENTLEMAN As I learned,
3 The night before there was no purpose in them
Of this remove.
KENT Hail to thee, noble master.
LEAR Ha!
Mak'st thou this shame thy pastime?
KENT No, my lord.
7 FOOL Ha, ha, he wears cruel garters. Horses are tied by
the heads, dogs and bears by th' neck, monkeys by th'
9 loins, and men by th' legs. When a man's overlusty at
10 legs, then he wears wooden netherstocks.
LEAR
What's he that hath so much thy place mistook
To set thee here?
KENT It is both he and she,
13 Your son and daughter.
LEAR No.
KENT Yes.
LEAR No, I say.
KENT I say yea.
[LEAR No, no, they would not.
KENT Yes, they have.]
LEAR
20 By Jupiter, I swear no!
KENT
21 By Juno, I swear ay!

II.4 3–4 *there . . . remove* they had no intention of leaving 7 *cruel* punning on "crewel," worsted cloth 9 *overlusty . . . legs* too eager to run 10 *netherstocks* stockings 13 *son* i.e., son-in-law 21 *Juno* queen of the gods, wife of Jupiter

LEAR They durst not do't;
They could not, would not do't. 'Tis worse than murder
To do upon respect such violent outrage. 23
Resolve me with all modest haste which way 24
Thou might'st deserve or they impose this usage,
Coming from us.

KENT My lord, when at their home
I did commend your highness' letters to them, 27
Ere I was risen from the place that showed
My duty kneeling, came there a reeking post, 29
Stewed in his haste, half breathless, panting forth 30
From Goneril his mistress salutations;
Delivered letters, spite of intermission, 32
Which presently they read; on whose contents 33
They summoned up their meiny, straight took horse, 34
Commanded me to follow and attend
The leisure of their answer, gave me cold looks;
And meeting here the other messenger,
Whose welcome I perceived had poisoned mine,
Being the very fellow which of late
Displayed so saucily against your highness, 40
Having more man that wit about me, drew; 41
He raised the house with loud and coward cries.
Your son and daughter found this trespass worth
The shame which here it suffers.

FOOL Winter's not gone yet, if the wild geese fly that way. 45
Fathers that wear rags
Do make their children blind, 48

---

23 *upon respect* to one who should be respected (as the king's messenger) **24** *Resolve* explain to; *modest* decent **27** *commend* deliver **29–30** *reeking . . . Stewed* hot and sweaty messenger **32** *spite . . . intermission* though he was interrupting me **33** *presently* immediately **34** *meiny* retinue **40** *Displayed* behaved **41** *wit* sense; *drew* drew my sword **45** *Winter's . . . way* if the geese are flying south ("that way," the way they fly in winter), winter's not over yet; i.e., things will get worse **48** *blind* (to their father's needs)

49 But fathers that bear bags
50 Shall see their children kind.
Fortune, that arrant whore,
52 Ne'er turns the key to th' poor.
53 But for all this, thou shalt have as many dolors for thy
54 daughters as thou canst tell in a year.

LEAR

55 O, how this mother swells up toward my heart!
56 *Hysterica passio,* down, thou climbing sorrow;
57 Thy element's below. Where is this daughter?

KENT

With the earl, sir, here within.

LEAR *[To Gentleman]* Follow me not;
Stay here. *Exit.*

GENTLEMAN

60 Made you no more offense but what you speak of?

KENT None.
How chance the king comes with so small a number?

63 FOOL An thou hadst been set i' th' stocks for that question, thou'dst well deserved it.

KENT Why, fool?

66 FOOL We'll set thee to school to an ant, to teach thee there's no laboring i' th' winter. All that follow their noses are led by their eyes but blind men, and there's not a nose among twenty but can smell him that's
70 stinking. Let go thy hold when a great wheel runs down a hill, lest it break thy neck with following. But the great one that goes upward, let him draw thee after. When a wise man gives thee better counsel, give me

---

49 *bags* moneybags **52** *turns the key* opens the door **53** *dolors* sorrows (punning on "dollars," the international European currency) **54** *tell* count **55** *mother* hysteria **56** *Hysterica passio* the medical term for hysteria **57** *Thy . . . below* (hysteria's natural place [*element*] was said to be the abdomen or, in women, the womb) **63** *An* if **66–67** *We'll . . . winter* (ants proverbially do not work in winter – implying that working for Lear is now unprofitable)

mine again. I would have none but knaves follow it 74
since a fool gives it.
That sir which serves and seeks for gain,
And follows but for form, 77
Will pack when it begins to rain 78
And leave thee in the storm.
But I will tarry; the fool will stay, 80
And let the wise man fly.
The knave turns fool that runs away; 82
The fool no knave, perdy. 83

KENT Where learned you this, fool?

FOOL Not i' th' stocks, fool.

Enter Lear and Gloucester.

LEAR

Deny to speak with me? They are sick, they are weary,
They have traveled all the night? Mere fetches, 87
The images of revolt and flying off! 88
Fetch me a better answer.

GLOUCESTER My dear lord,
You know the fiery quality of the duke, 90
How unremovable and fixed he is
In his own course.

LEAR

Vengeance, plague, death, confusion!
Fiery? What quality? Why, Gloucester, Gloucester,
I'd speak with the Duke of Cornwall and his wife.

GLOUCESTER

Well, my good lord, I have informed them so.

LEAR

Informed them? Dost thou understand me, man?

GLOUCESTER Ay, my good lord.

LEAR

The king would speak with Cornwall. The dear father

---

74 *again* back **77** *form* show **78** *pack* leave **82** *knave . . . away* i.e., disloyalty is the real folly **83** *perdy* by God (French *pardieu*) **87** *fetches* pretenses **88** *images* signs; *flying off* insurrection **90** *quality* disposition

100 Would with his daughter speak, commands – tends –
service.
Are they informed of this? My breath and blood!
Fiery? The fiery duke, tell the hot duke that –
No, but not yet. Maybe he is not well.
104 Infirmity doth still neglect all office
105 Whereto our health is bound. We are not ourselves
When nature, being oppressed, commands the mind
To suffer with the body. I'll forbear;
108 And am fallen out with my more headier will
109 To take the indisposed and sickly fit
110 For the sound man. – Death on my state! Wherefore
111 Should he sit here? This act persuades me
112 That this remotion of the duke and her
113 Is practice only. Give me my servant forth.
Go tell the duke and's wife I'd speak with them!
115 Now, presently! Bid them come forth and hear me,
Or at their chamber door I'll beat the drum
117 Till it cry sleep to death.

GLOUCESTER
I would have all well betwixt you. *Exit.*

LEAR
O me, my heart, my rising heart! But down!

120 FOOL Cry to it, nuncle, as the cockney did to the eels
121 when she put 'em i' th' paste alive. She knapped 'em o'
122 th' coxcombs with a stick and cried, "Down, wantons,

---

100 *tends – service* awaits their obedience **104** *still . . . office* always neglects duty **105** *Whereto . . . bound* which in health we are bound to obey **108** *fallen out* angry; *headier* headstrong **109** *To take* that mistook **110** *Death . . . state* (the expletive is ironic: "Let my royal power die") **111** *he* Kent **112** *remotion* either removal (from their home) or aloofness (from Lear) **113** *practice* trickery; *Give . . . forth* release my servant **115** *presently* instantly **117** *Till . . . death* till it kills sleep with the noise **120** *cockney* Londoner (i.e., a city dweller) **121** *paste* pastry **121–22** *knapped 'em o' th' coxcombs* knocked them on the head **122** *wantons* rascals, with a quibble on lechers and on deflating erections

down!" 'Twas her brother that, in pure kindness to his
horse, buttered his hay. 124

Enter Cornwall, Regan, Gloucester, Servants.

LEAR

Good morrow to you both.

CORNWALL Hail to your grace.

Kent here set at liberty.

REGAN

I am glad to see your highness.

LEAR

Regan, I think you are. I know what reason
I have to think so. If thou shouldst not be glad,
I would divorce me from thy mother's tomb,
Sepulch'ring an adult'ress. *[To Kent]* O, are you free? 130
Some other time for that. – Beloved Regan,
Thy sister's naught. O Regan, she hath tied 132
Sharp-toothed unkindness, like a vulture, here.
I can scarce speak to thee. Thou'lt not believe
With how depraved a quality – O Regan!

REGAN

I pray you, sir, take patience. I have hope
You less know how to value her desert 137
Than she to scant her duty.

LEAR Say? How is that?

REGAN

I cannot think my sister in the least
Would fail her obligation. If, sir, perchance *140*
She have restrained the riots of your followers,
'Tis on such ground, and to such wholesome end,
As clears her from all blame.

---

124 *buttered . . . hay* (another example of misguided kindness: horses will not eat grease) **130** *Sepulch'ring . . . adult'ress* i.e., it would prove you were not my daughter **132** *naught* wicked (cf. naughty) **137–38** *You . . . duty* the problem is that you are unable to evaluate her merit rather than that she has failed in her duty

LEAR
My curses on her!
REGAN O, sir, you are old;
145 Nature in you stands on the very verge
Of his confine. You should be ruled, and led
147 By some discretion that discerns your state
Better than you yourself. Therefore I pray you
That to our sister you do make return;
150 Say you have wronged her.
LEAR Ask her forgiveness?
151 Do you but mark how this becomes the house:
"Dear daughter, I confess that I am old.
[Kneels.]
153 Age is unnecessary. On my knees I beg
That you'll vouchsafe me raiment, bed, and food."
REGAN
Good sir, no more. These are unsightly tricks.
Return you to my sister.
LEAR *[Rises.]* Never, Regan.
157 She hath abated me of half my train,
Looked black upon me, struck me with her tongue
Most serpentlike upon the very heart.
160 All the stored vengeances of heaven fall
161 On her ingrateful top! Strike her young bones,
162 You taking airs, with lameness.
CORNWALL Fie, sir, fie!
LEAR
You nimble lightnings, dart your blinding flames
Into her scornful eyes! Infect her beauty,
165 You fen-sucked fogs drawn by the pow'rful sun
To fall and blister –

145–46 *Nature . . . confine* your life stands at the very edge of its allotted space **147** *discretion . . . state* discerning person who understands your condition **151** *house* family **153** *Age is* old people are **157** *abated* deprived **161** *top* head **162** *taking airs* infectious vapors **165** *fen-sucked . . . sun* (the sun was believed to draw infectious vapors from swamps)

REGAN O the blessed gods!
So will you wish on me when the rash mood is on.
LEAR
No, Regan, thou shalt never have my curse.
Thy tender-hefted nature shall not give 169
Thee o'er to harshness. Her eyes are fierce, but thine *170*
Do comfort, and not burn. 'Tis not in thee
To grudge my pleasures, to cut off my train,
To bandy hasty words, to scant my sizes, 173
And, in conclusion, to oppose the bolt 174
Against my coming in. Thou better know'st
The offices of nature, bond of childhood, 176
Effects of courtesy, dues of gratitude. 177
Thy half o' th' kingdom hast thou not forgot,
Wherein I thee endowed. 179
REGAN Good sir, to th' purpose.
Tucket within.
LEAR
Who put my man i' th' stocks? *180*
CORNWALL What trumpet's that?
REGAN
I know't – my sister's. This approves her letter 182
That she would soon be here.
Enter Steward [Oswald]. Is your lady come?
LEAR
This is a slave, whose easy-borrowed pride 184
Dwells in the fickle grace of her he follows.
Out, varlet, from my sight. 186
CORNWALL What means your grace?
LEAR
Who stocked my servant? Regan, I have good hope

---

169 *tender-hefted* gently disposed **173** *sizes* allowance **174** *oppose the bolt* bolt the door **176** *offices* duties **177** *Effects* obligations **179** *to . . . purpose* get to the point **182** *approves* confirms **184** *easy-borrowed* impudently assumed **186** *varlet* scoundrel

188 Thou didst not know on't.
Enter Goneril. Who comes here? O heavens!
189 If you do love old men, if your sweet sway
190 Allow obedience, if you yourselves are old,
Make it your cause. Send down, and take my part.
[To Goneril]
Art not ashamed to look upon this beard?
O Regan, will you take her by the hand?

GONERIL
Why not by th' hand, sir? How have I offended?
195 All's not offense that indiscretion finds
196 And dotage terms so.

LEAR O sides, you are too tough!
Will you yet hold? How came my man i' th' stocks?

CORNWALL
I set him there, sir; but his own disorders
199 Deserved much less advancement.

LEAR You? Did you?

REGAN
200 I pray you, father, being weak, seem so.
If till the expiration of your month
You will return and sojourn with my sister,
Dismissing half your train, come then to me.
204 I am now from home, and out of that provision
205 Which shall be needful for your entertainment.

LEAR
Return to her, and fifty men dismissed?
No, rather I abjure all roofs, and choose
208 To wage against the enmity o' th' air,
To be a comrade with the wolf and owl,
210 Necessity's sharp pinch. Return with her?
Why, the hot-blooded France, that dowerless took

---

188 *on't* of it **189–90** *If . . . obedience* if you permit gentle rule to be obeyed **195** *indiscretion* poor judgment **196** *sides* breast (which should burst with grief) **199** *less advancement* less of a promotion – i.e., a worse punishment **204** *from* away from **205** *entertainment* reception **208** *wage* fight

Our youngest born, I could as well be brought
To knee his throne, and, squirelike, pension beg 213
To keep base life afoot. Return with her?
Persuade me rather to be slave and sumpter 215
To this detested groom.

GONERIL At your choice, sir.

LEAR

I prithee, daughter, do not make me mad.
I will not trouble thee, my child; farewell.
We'll no more meet, no more see one another.
But yet thou art my flesh, my blood, my daughter – *220*
Or rather a disease that's in my flesh,
Which I must needs call mine. Thou art a boil,
A plague-sore, or embossèd carbuncle 223
In my corrupted blood. But I'll not chide thee.
Let shame come when it will, I do not call it.
I do not bid the thunder-bearer shoot, 226
Nor tell tales of thee to high-judging Jove.
Mend when thou canst, be better at thy leisure;
I can be patient, I can stay with Regan,
I and my hundred knights. *230*

REGAN

Not altogether so.
I looked not for you yet, nor am provided
For your fit welcome. Give ear, sir, to my sister;
For those that mingle reason with your passion 234
Must be content to think you old and so –
But she knows what she does.

LEAR Is this well spoken?

REGAN

I dare avouch it, sir. What, fifty followers? 237
Is it not well? What should you need of more?
Yea, or so many, sith that both charge and danger 239

---

213 *knee* kneel to **215** *sumpter* packhorse **223** *embossèd carbuncle* swollen tumor **226** *the thunder-bearer* Jove **234** *mingle . . . passion* deal rationally with your intemperate behavior **237** *avouch* swear **239** *sith that* since; *charge* expense

240 Speak 'gainst so great a number? How in one house
Should many people, under two commands,
Hold amity? 'Tis hard, almost impossible.

GONERIL

Why might not you, my lord, receive attendance
From those that she calls servants, or from mine?

REGAN

245 Why not, my lord? If then they chanced to slack ye,
We could control them. If you will come to me
(For now I spy a danger), I entreat you
To bring but five-and-twenty. To no more
249 Will I give place or notice.

LEAR

250 I gave you all.

REGAN And in good time you gave it.

LEAR

251 Made you my guardians, my depositaries,
252 But kept a reservation to be followed
With such a number. What, must I come to you
With five-and-twenty? Regan, said you so?

REGAN

And speak't again, my lord. No more with me.

LEAR

256 Those wicked creatures yet do look well-favored
When others are more wicked; not being the worst
258 Stands in some rank of praise.
[To Goneril] I'll go with thee.
Thy fifty yet doth double five-and-twenty,
260 And thou art twice her love.

GONERIL Hear me, my lord.
What need you five-and-twenty? ten? or five?
To follow in a house where twice so many
Have a command to tend you?

---

245 *slack* neglect **249** *notice* recognition **251** *depositaries* trustees **252** *kept . . . be* stipulated that I be **256** *well-favored* attractive **258** *Stands . . . of* deserves at least some **260** *twice . . . love* twice as loving as she

REGAN What need one?

LEAR

O reason not the need! Our basest beggars 264
Are in the poorest thing superfluous. 265
Allow not nature more than nature needs, 266
Man's life is cheap as beast's. Thou art a lady:
If only to go warm were gorgeous, 268
Why, nature needs not what thou gorgeous wear'st,
Which scarcely keeps thee warm. But, for true need – *270*
You heavens, give me that patience, patience I need.
You see me here, you gods, a poor old man,
As full of grief as age, wretched in both.
If it be you that stirs these daughters' hearts
Against their father, fool me not so much 275
To bear it tamely; touch me with noble anger,
And let not women's weapons, waterdrops,
Stain my man's cheeks. No, you unnatural hags!
I will have such revenges on you both
That all the world shall – I will do such things – *280*
What they are, yet I know not; but they shall be
The terrors of the earth. You think I'll weep.
No, I'll not weep.
Storm and tempest.
I have full cause of weeping, but this heart
Shall break into a hundred thousand flaws 285
Or ere I'll weep. O fool, I shall go mad! 286
Exeunt [Lear, Fool, Kent, and Gloucester].

CORNWALL

Let us withdraw; 'twill be a storm.

REGAN

This house is little; the old man and's people
Cannot be well bestowed.

---

264 *reason* calculate **265** *Are . . . superfluous* have something more than is absolutely necessary **266** *Allow not* if you do not grant **268** *If . . . gorgeous* if warmth were the measure of fashionable dress **275–76** *fool . . . To* don't make me such a fool as to **285** *flaws* fragments **286** *Or ere* before

GONERIL
290 'Tis his own blame; hath put himself from rest
And must needs taste his folly.
REGAN
292 For his particular, I'll receive him gladly,
But not one follower.
GONERIL So am I purposed.
Where is my Lord of Gloucester?
CORNWALL
Followed the old man forth.
[Enter Gloucester.] He is returned.
GLOUCESTER
The king is in high rage.
CORNWALL Whither is he going?
GLOUCESTER
He calls to horse, but will I know not whither.
CORNWALL
'Tis best to give him way; he leads himself.
GONERIL
My lord, entreat him by no means to stay.
GLOUCESTER
300 Alack, the night comes on, and the high winds
301 Do sorely ruffle. For many miles about
There's scarce a bush.
REGAN O, sir, to willful men
The injuries that they themselves procure
Must be their schoolmasters. Shut up your doors.
305 He is attended with a desperate train,
306 And what they may incense him to, being apt
To have his ear abused, wisdom bids fear.
CORNWALL
Shut up your doors, my lord; 'tis a wild night.
My Regan counsels well. Come out o' th' storm.
Exeunt.

---

292 *his particular* himself alone **301** *ruffle* rage **305** *desperate train* violent troop **306–7** *apt . . . abused* i.e., likely to be misled

*

❧ III.1 *Storm still. Enter Kent [disguised] and a Gentleman severally.*

KENT
Who's there besides foul weather?
GENTLEMAN
One minded like the weather, most unquietly.
KENT
I know you. Where's the king?
GENTLEMAN
Contending with the fretful elements; 4
Bids the wind blow the earth into the sea,
Or swell the curlèd waters 'bove the main, 6
That things might change or cease; [tears his white hair,
Which the impetuous blasts, with eyeless rage, 8
Catch in their fury and make nothing of;
Strives in his little world of man to outscorn *10*
The to-and-fro-conflicting wind and rain.
This night, wherein the cub-drawn bear would couch, 12
The lion and the belly-pinchèd wolf 13
Keep their fur dry, unbonneted he runs,
And bids what will take all.] 15
KENT But who is with him?
GENTLEMAN
None but the fool, who labors to outjest 16
His heart-struck injuries.
KENT Sir, I do know you,
And dare upon the warrant of my note 18

III.1 A heath **s.d.** *severally* at different doors **4** *fretful elements* angry weather **6** *main* mainland **8** *eyeless* blind **12** *cub-drawn* sucked dry by her cub, and therefore ravenous; *couch* stay inside **13** *belly-pinchèd* starving **15** *bids . . . will* commands whatever wishes to **16** *outjest* overcome with jesting **18** *my note* what I have observed about you

Commend a dear thing to you. There is division,
Although as yet the face of it is covered
With mutual cunning, 'twixt Albany and Cornwall;
Who have – as who have not, that their great stars
Throned and set high? – servants, who seem no less,
Which are to France the spies and speculations
Intelligent of our state. What hath been seen,
Either in snuffs and packings of the dukes,
Or the hard rein which both of them have borne
Against the old kind king, or something deeper,
Whereof, perchance, these are but furnishings –
[But, true it is, from France there comes a power
Into this scattered kingdom, who already,
Wise in our negligence, have secret feet
In some of our best ports and are at point
To show their open banner. Now to you:
If on my credit you dare build so far
To make your speed to Dover, you shall find
Some that will thank you, making just report
Of how unnatural and bemadding sorrow
The king hath cause to plain.
I am a gentleman of blood and breeding,
And from some knowledge and assurance offer
This office to you.]

GENTLEMAN
I will talk further with you.

KENT No, do not.
For confirmation that I am much more
Than my outwall, open this purse and take
What it contains. If you shall see Cordelia,

---

19 *Commend . . . thing* entrust a precious matter; *division* dissension 22 *that . . . stars* whom destiny has 23 *who . . . less* i.e., who really appear to be servants 24–25 *speculations / Intelligent* observant informers 26 *snuffs and packings* quarrels and intrigues 27 *hard rein* harsh treatment; *borne* used 29 *furnishings* pretexts 32 *Wise in* knowing of; *secret feet* secretly set foot 33 *at point* ready 35 *If . . . build* if you trust me 39 *plain* complain 42 *office* undertaking 45 *outwall* outward appearance

As fear not but you shall, show her this ring,
And she will tell you who that fellow is 48
That yet you do not know. Fie on this storm!
I will go seek the king. 50

GENTLEMAN
Give me your hand. Have you no more to say?

KENT
Few words, but, to effect, more than all yet: 52
That when we have found the king – in which your pain 53
That way, I'll this – he that first lights on him
Holla the other. *Exeunt [severally].*

*

❧ III.2 *Storm still. Enter Lear and Fool.*

LEAR
Blow, winds, and crack your cheeks! Rage, blow! 1
You cataracts and hurricanoes, spout 2
Till you have drenched our steeples, drowned the cocks. 3
You sulph'rous and thought-executing fires, 4
Vaunt-couriers of oak-cleaving thunderbolts, 5
Singe my white head. And thou, all-shaking thunder,
Strike flat the thick rotundity o' th' world,
Crack nature's molds, all germens spill at once, 8
That makes ingrateful man.

FOOL O nuncle, court holy water in a dry house is better than this rainwater out o' door. Good nuncle, in; ask thy daughters blessing. Here's a night pities neither wise men nor fools. 10

---

48 *who . . . is* i.e., who I am 52 *to effect* in importance 53–54 *your . . . way* in your efforts, go that way

III.2 Elsewhere on the heath 1 *crack . . . cheeks* (as winds are represented on old maps, heads with cheeks puffed out) 2 *cataracts . . . hurricanoes* torrential rains and hurricanes 3 *cocks* weather vanes 4 *thought-executing* either annihilating thought or acting as fast as thought 5 *Vaunt-couriers* heralds 8 *Nature's molds* (in which life is given form); *germens* seeds 10 *court holy water* flattery

LEAR
Rumble thy bellyful. Spit, fire. Spout, rain.
Nor rain, wind, thunder, fire are my daughters.
16 I tax not you, you elements, with unkindness.
I never gave you kingdom, called you children;
18 You owe me no subscription. Then let fall
Your horrible pleasure. Here I stand your slave,
20 A poor, infirm, weak, and despised old man.
21 But yet I call you servile ministers,
That will with two pernicious daughters join
23 Your high-engendered battles 'gainst a head
So old and white as this. O, ho! 'tis foul.
FOOL He that has a house to put's head in has a good
26 headpiece.
27 The codpiece that will house
Before the head has any,
29 The head and he shall louse:
30 So beggars marry many.
31 The man that makes his toe
What he his heart should make
Shall of a corn cry woe,
And turn his sleep to wake.
35 For there was never yet fair woman but she made mouths in a glass.
Enter Kent [disguised].
LEAR
No, I will be the pattern of all patience;
I will say nothing. *[He sits.]*
KENT Who's there?

---

16 *tax* charge **18** *subscription* deference **21** *ministers* agents **23** *high-engendered battles* heavenly batallions **26** *headpiece* both helmet and brain **27** *codpiece* the pouch for the genitals on men's breeches, here used for the penis; *house* lodge (in copulation) **29–30** *The . . . many* will infest both the head and the codpiece with lice, and end in married poverty **31–32** *The . . . make* (a parallel instance of preferring the lower part to the higher) **35–36** *made . . . glass* practiced smiling in a mirror – i.e., was afflicted with vanity

FOOL Marry, here's grace and a codpiece; that's a wise man and a fool. 40

KENT

Alas, sir, are you here? Things that love night
Love not such nights as these. The wrathful skies
Gallow the very wanderers of the dark 44
And make them keep their caves. Since I was man, 45
Such sheets of fire, such bursts of horrid thunder,
Such groans of roaring wind and rain, I never
Remember to have heard. Man's nature cannot carry 48
Th' affliction nor the fear.

LEAR Let the great gods
That keep this dreadful pudder o'er our heads 50
Find out their enemies now. Tremble, thou wretch,
That hast within thee undivulgèd crimes
Unwhipped of justice. Hide thee, thou bloody hand, 53
Thou perjured, and thou simular of virtue 54
That art incestuous. Caitiff, to pieces shake, 55
That under covert and convenient seeming 56
Has practiced on man's life. Close pent-up guilts, 57
Rive your concealing continents and cry 58
These dreadful summoners grace. I am a man
More sinned against than sinning. 60

KENT Alack, bareheaded?
Gracious my lord, hard by here is a hovel; 61
Some friendship will it lend you 'gainst the tempest.
Repose you there, while I to this hard house
(More harder than the stones whereof 'tis raised,
Which even but now, demanding after you, 65

---

40 *Marry* (a mild exclamation, originally an oath on the name of the Virgin) **44** *Gallow* frighten **45** *keep* stay inside **48** *carry* endure **50** *pudder* tumult **53** *of* by **54** *simular of* pretender to **55** *Caitiff* wretch **56** *seeming* hypocrisy **57** *practiced on* plotted against; *Close* secret **58** *Rive* split open **58–59** *cry . . . grace* beg for mercy from these terrible agents of justice (summoners are officers of church courts) **61** *hard* close **65** *demanding* as I was asking

Denied me to come in) return, and force
67 Their scanted courtesy.

LEAR

My wits begin to turn.
Come on, my boy. How dost, my boy? Art cold?
70 I am cold myself. Where is this straw, my fellow?
The art of our necessities is strange,
And can make vile things precious. Come, your hovel.
Poor fool and knave, I have one part in my heart
That's sorry yet for thee.

FOOL *[Sings.]*

75 He that has and a little tiny wit,
With, heigh-ho, the wind and the rain,
77 Must make content with his fortunes fit
78 Though the rain it raineth every day.

LEAR True, boy. Come, bring us to this hovel.

Exit [with Kent].

80 FOOL This is a brave night to cool a courtesan. I'll speak a prophecy ere I go:

82 When priests are more in word than matter;
83 When brewers mar their malt with water;
84 When nobles are their tailors' tutors,
85 No heretics burned, but wenches' suitors;
When every case in law is right,
No squire in debt nor no poor knight;
When slanders do not live in tongues,
89 Nor cutpurses come not to throngs;
90 When usurers tell their gold i' th' field,
And bawds and whores do churches build –

---

67 *scanted* deficient **75** *and* only, even **75–78** (The song refigures Feste's song at the end of *Twelfth Night*.) **77** *make . . . fit* be content with his lot **80** *brave . . . courtesan* fine night to cool off the lust of a prostitute **82** *more . . . matter* preach better than they practice **83** *mar* dilute **84** *are . . . tutors* teach tailors about fashion (i.e., know what they want) **85** *No . . . suitors* either the only people who burn are lovers (who burn with passion) or the only heretics who burn are faithless lovers (who burn with venereal disease) **89** *cutpurses* pickpockets **90** *tell . . . field* count their money openly (because they have nothing to hide)

Then shall the realm of Albion 92
Come to great confusion.
Then comes the time, who lives to see't,
That going shall be used with feet. 95
This prophecy Merlin shall make, for I live before his time. *Exit.*

*

❧ III.3 *Enter Gloucester and Edmund.*

GLOUCESTER Alack, alack, Edmund, I like not this unnatural dealing. When I desired their leave that I might pity him, they took from me the use of mine own 3
house, charged me on pain of perpetual displeasure neither to speak of him, entreat for him, or any way sustain him.

EDMUND Most savage and unnatural.

GLOUCESTER Go to; say you nothing. There is division 8
between the dukes, and a worse matter than that. I
have received a letter this night – 'tis dangerous to be 10
spoken – I have locked the letter in my closet. These 11
injuries the king now bears will be revenged home; 12
there is part of a power already footed; we must incline 13
to the king. I will look him and privily relieve him. Go 14
you and maintain talk with the duke, that my charity
be not of him perceived. If he ask for me, I am ill and 16
gone to bed. If I die for it, as no less is threatened me,
the king my old master must be relieved. There is
strange things toward, Edmund; pray you be careful. 19
Exit.

---

92 *Albion* England 95 *going . . . feet* walking will be done on foot (i.e., things will be just as they are now)

III.3 Gloucester's house 3 *pity* take pity on 8 *Go to* be quiet 11 *closet* (any private room: study, bedroom) 12 *home* thoroughly 13 *power* army; *footed* landed; *incline* to side with 14 *look* search for; *privily* secretly 16 *of* by 19 *toward* impending

EDMUND

20 This courtesy forbid thee shall the duke
Instantly know, and of that letter too.
22 This seems a fair deserving, and must draw me
That which my father loses – no less than all.
The younger rises when the old doth fall. *Exit.*

*

~ III.4 *Enter Lear, Kent [disguised], and Fool.*

KENT

Here is the place, my lord. Good my lord, enter.
The tyranny of the open night's too rough
3 For nature to endure.
Storm still.

LEAR Let me alone.

KENT Good my lord, enter here.

LEAR Wilt break my heart?

KENT

I had rather break mine own. Good my lord, enter.

LEAR

Thou think'st 'tis much that this contentious storm
Invades us to the skin. So 'tis to thee,
10 But where the greater malady is fixed
The lesser is scarce felt. Thou'dst shun a bear;
But if thy flight lay toward the roaring sea,
13 Thou'dst meet the bear i' th' mouth. When the mind's free,
14 The body's delicate. The tempest in my mind
Doth from my senses take all feeling else
Save what beats there. Filial ingratitude,

---

20 *courtesy . . . thee* kindness you have been forbidden to show 22 *a fair deserving* an action that would deserve a fair reward

III.4 Before a hovel on the heath 3 *nature* humanity, human frailty 10 *fixed* lodged 13 *i' th' mouth* head-on; *When . . . free* only when the mind is untroubled 14 *delicate* sensitive to pain

Is it not as this mouth should tear this hand 17
For lifting food to't? But I will punish home.
No, I will weep no more. In such a night
To shut me out! Pour on; I will endure. *20*
In such a night as this! O Regan, Goneril,
Your old kind father, whose frank heart gave all –
O, that way madness lies; let me shun that.
No more of that.

KENT Good my lord, enter here.

LEAR
Prithee go in thyself; seek thine own ease.
This tempest will not give me leave to ponder
On things would hurt me more, but I'll go in. 27
[To the Fool]
In, boy; go first. You houseless poverty –
Nay, get thee in. I'll pray, and then I'll sleep.
Exit [Fool].
Poor naked wretches, wheresoe'er you are, *30*
That bide the pelting of this pitiless storm, 31
How shall your houseless heads and unfed sides,
Your looped and windowed raggedness, defend you 33
From seasons such as these? O, I have ta'en 34
Too little care of this! Take physic, pomp; 35
Expose thyself to feel what wretches feel,
That thou mayst shake the superflux to them 37
And show the heavens more just.

EDGAR *[Within]* Fathom and half, fathom and half! 39
Poor Tom! *40*
Enter Fool.

FOOL Come not in here, nuncle; here's a spirit. Help me, help me!

---

17 *as* as if 27 *would* that would 31 *bide* endure, wait out 33 *looped, windowed* both mean *full of holes* 34 *seasons* weather 35 *Take . . . pomp* grandeur, purge yourself 37 *shake . . . superflux* pour out your surplus 39 *Fathom . . . half* nine feet of water (the call of a sailor taking soundings)

KENT
Give me thy hand. Who's there?
FOOL A spirit, a spirit. He says his name's poor Tom.
KENT
What are thou that dost grumble there i' th' straw?
Come forth.
Enter Edgar [as Tom o' Bedlam].
47 EDGAR Away! the foul fiend follows me. Through the sharp hawthorn blow the winds. Hum! go to thy bed and warm thee.
50 LEAR Didst thou give all to thy daughters? And art thou come to this?
EDGAR Who gives anything to poor Tom? whom the foul fiend hath led through fire and through flame, through ford and whirlpool, o'er bog and quagmire;
55 that hath laid knives under his pillow and halters in his
56 pew, set ratsbane by his porridge, made him proud of heart, to ride on a bay trotting horse over four-inched
58 bridges, to course his own shadow for a traitor. Bless
59 thy five wits, Tom's acold. O, do, de, do, de, do, de.
60 Bless thee from whirlwinds, star-blasting, and taking. Do poor Tom some charity, whom the foul fiend vexes. There could I have him now – and there – and there again – and there –
Storm still.
LEAR
Has his daughters brought him to this pass?
Couldst thou save nothing? Wouldst thou give 'em all?
FOOL Nay, he reserved a blanket, else we had been all shamed.

47–48 *Through . . . winds* (apparently a fragment of a ballad, quoted again at l. 99) **55–56** *knives, halters, ratsbane* (all temptations to suicide); *halters . . . pew* nooses on his balcony **56–58** *made . . . bridges* i.e., made him take mad risks **58** *course . . . traitor* hunt his own shadow as if it were an enemy **59** *five wits* the constituent parts of intelligence in Renaissance theories of cognition: common wit, imagination, fantasy, estimation, memory **60** *star-blasting, taking* malignant stars, infection

LEAR
Now all the plagues that in the pendulous air 68
Hang fated o'er men's faults light on thy daughters! 69
KENT He hath no daughters, sir. *70*
LEAR
Death, traitor! Nothing could have subdued nature
To such a lowness but his unkind daughters.
Is it the fashion that discarded fathers
Should have thus little mercy on their flesh?
Judicious punishment – 'twas this flesh begot
Those pelican daughters. 76
EDGAR Pillicock sat on Pillicock Hill. Alow, alow, loo, 77
loo!
FOOL This cold night will turn us all to fools and mad-
men. *80*
EDGAR Take heed o' th' foul fiend; obey thy parents; 81
keep thy words' justice; swear not; commit not with 82
man's sworn spouse; set not thy sweet heart on proud 83
array. Tom's acold.
LEAR What hast thou been?
EDGAR A servingman, proud in heart and mind; that
curled my hair, wore gloves in my cap; served the lust
of my mistress' heart, and did the act of darkness with 87
her; swore as many oaths as I spake words, and broke
them in the sweet face of heaven. One that slept in the 90
contriving of lust, and waked to do it. Wine loved I
deeply, dice dearly; and in woman out-paramoured the 92

---

68 *pendulous* overhanging **69** *fated* ominously **76** *pelican* cannibalistic (young pelicans were said to feed on their mother's blood) **77–78** *Pillicock . . . loo* a fragment of a nursery rhyme; *pillicock* = both an endearment and baby talk for penis **81** *Take heed* beware; *obey . . . parents* this and the following injunctions are from the Ten Commandments **82** *keep . . . justice* i.e., do not lie **82–83** *commit not . . . spouse* i.e., do not commit adultery **83–84** *proud array* luxurious clothing **87** *wore . . . cap* as courtly lovers did with tokens from their mistresses **90–91** *slept . . . lust* went to sleep planning acts of lechery **92–93** *out-paramoured . . . Turk* had more lovers than the Sultan has in his harem

93 Turk. False of heart, light of ear, bloody of hand; hog in
sloth, fox in stealth, wolf in greediness, dog in madness,
95 lion in prey. Let not the creaking of shoes nor the
rustling of silks betray thy poor heart to woman. Keep
97 thy foot out of brothels, thy hand out of plackets, thy
98 pen from lenders' books, and defy the foul fiend. Still
through the hawthorn blows the cold wind; says suum,
100 mun, nonny. Dolphin my boy, boy, sessa! let him
trot by.

Storm still.

102 LEAR Thou wert better in a grave than to answer with
thy uncovered body this extremity of the skies. Is man
no more than this? Consider him well. Thou ow'st the
worm no silk, the beast no hide, the sheep no wool, the
106 cat no perfume. Ha! here's three on's are sophisticated.
107 Thou art the thing itself; unaccommodated man is no
more but such a poor, bare, forked animal as thou art.
109 Off, off, you lendings! Come, unbutton here.

[Begins to disrobe.]

110 FOOL Prithee, nuncle, be contented; 'tis a naughty night
to swim in. Now a little fire in a wild field were like an
old lecher's heart – a small spark, all the rest on's body
cold. Look, here comes a walking fire.

Enter Gloucester with a torch.

114 EDGAR This is the foul Flibbertigibbet. He begins at
115 curfew, and walks till the first cock. He gives the web
116 and the pin, squints the eye, and makes the harelip;

---

93 *light of ear* attentive to gossip and slander **95–96** *creaking . . . silks* (both fashionable in women) **97** *plackets* slits in women's skirts (hence vaginas) **98** *pen . . . books* i.e., stay out of debt **100** *Dolphin . . . sessa* (Unexplained; possibly a bit of a ballad, possibly a hunting call. Dolphin is usually taken to refer to the French crown prince, the dauphin, but it sounds more like a hunting dog's name; *sessa* [French *cessez*] = stop) **102** *answer* experience **106** *cat* civet cat, from whose secretions perfume was made; *on's* of us; *sophisticated* artificial **107** *unaccommodated* unadorned, unfurnished **109** *lendings* borrowed articles (because not part of his body) **110** *naughty* evil **114** *Flibbertigibbet* (in Elizabethan folklore, a dancing devil) **115** *curfew* 9 P.M.; *first cock* midnight **115–16** *the . . . pin* eye cataracts **116** *squints* makes squint

mildews the white wheat, and hurts the poor creature 117
of earth.
[Sings.]
Swithold footed thrice the 'old; 119
He met the nightmare, and her ninefold; 120
Bid her alight 121
And her troth plight, 122
And aroint thee, witch, aroint thee! 123

KENT How fares your grace?
LEAR *[Pointing to Gloucester]* What's he?
KENT *[To Gloucester]* Who's there? What is't you seek?
GLOUCESTER What are you there? Your names?
EDGAR Poor Tom, that eats the swimming frog, the
toad, the tadpole, the wall newt and the water; that in 129
the fury of his heart, when the foul fiend rages, eats cow *130*
dung for sallets, swallows the old rat and the ditch dog, 131
drinks the green mantle of the standing pool; who is 132
whipped from tithing to tithing, and stock-punished 133
and imprisoned; who hath had three suits to his back,
six shirts to his body,

Horse to ride, and weapon to wear,
But mice and rats, and such small deer, 137
Have been Tom's food for seven long year.

Beware my follower! Peace, Smulkin, peace, thou fiend! 139

---

117 *white* almost ripe **119** *Swithold* Saint Withold (invoked as a general protector against harm); *footed . . . 'old* walked the plain (wold) three times **120** *nightmare* incubus, female demon; *ninefold* nine offspring **121** *Bid . . . alight* ordered her to get off (the sleeper's chest) **122** *her troth plight* give her promise (not to do it again) **123** *aroint thee* be gone **129** *wall newt* wall lizard; *water* i.e., water newt (an aquatic salamander) **131** *sallets* delicacies; *ditch dog* dead dog thrown in a ditch **132** *green mantle* scum; *standing* stagnant **133** *tithing* parish; *stock-punished* put in the stocks **137** *deer* game (the jingle is adapted from the popular romance *Bevis of Hampton*) **139** *Smulkin* (like Modo and Mahu on the following page, devil identified in Samuel Harsnett's *Declaration of Egregious Popish Impostures,* 1603)

GLOUCESTER
140 What, hath your grace no better company?
EDGAR
The prince of darkness is a gentleman.
Modo he's called, and Mahu.
GLOUCESTER
Our flesh and blood, my lord, is grown so vile
144 That it doth hate what gets it.
EDGAR Poor Tom's acold.
GLOUCESTER
146 Go in with me. My duty cannot suffer
T' obey in all your daughters' hard commands.
Though their injunction be to bar my doors
And let this tyrannous night take hold upon you,
150 Yet have I ventured to come seek you out
And bring you where both fire and food is ready.
LEAR
First let me talk with this philosopher. –
What is the cause of thunder?
KENT
Good my lord, take his offer; go into th' house.
LEAR
155 I'll talk a word with this same learnèd Theban. –
156 What is your study?
EDGAR
157 How to prevent the fiend, and to kill vermin.
LEAR
Let me ask you one word in private.
[They talk apart.]
KENT
Importune him once more to go, my lord.
160 His wits begin t' unsettle.

---

144 *gets* begets **146** *suffer* allow me **155** *learnèd Theban* Greek scholar **156** *study* field of study **157** *prevent* thwart

GLOUCESTER
Canst thou blame him?
Storm still.
His daughters seek his death. Ah, that good Kent,
He said it would be thus, poor banished man!
Thou sayest the king grows mad – I'll tell thee, friend,
I am almost mad myself. I had a son,
Now outlawed from my blood; he sought my life 166
But lately, very late. I loved him, friend, 167
No father his son dearer. True to tell thee,
The grief hath crazed my wits. What a night's this!
I do beseech your grace – *170*
LEAR
O, cry you mercy, sir. 171
Noble philosopher, your company.
EDGAR Tom's acold.
GLOUCESTER
In, fellow, there, into th' hovel; keep thee warm.
LEAR Come, let's in all.
KENT This way, my lord.
LEAR
With him!
I will keep still with my philosopher.
KENT
Good my lord, soothe him; let him take the fellow. 179
GLOUCESTER Take him you on. 180
KENT Sirrah, come on; go along with us.
LEAR Come, good Athenian. 182
GLOUCESTER No words, no words! Hush.

---

166 *outlawed . . . blood* disowned, disinherited **167** *late* recently **171** *cry . . . mercy* I beg your pardon **179** *soothe* humor **180** *you on* along with you **182** *Athenian* philosopher

184 EDGAR Child Roland to the dark tower came;
185 His word was still "Fie, foh, and fum,
I smell the blood of a British man." *Exeunt.*

*

❧ III.5 *Enter Cornwall and Edmund.*

CORNWALL I will have my revenge ere I depart his house.

3 EDMUND How, my lord, I may be censured, that nature
4 thus gives way to loyalty, something fears me to think of.

CORNWALL I now perceive it was not altogether your
7 brother's evil disposition made him seek his death; but
8 a provoking merit, set awork by a reprovable badness in
9 himself.

10 EDMUND How malicious is my fortune that I must repent to be just! This is the letter which he spoke of,
12 which approves him an intelligent party to the advantages of France. O heavens, that this treason were not or not I the detector!

CORNWALL Go with me to the duchess.

EDMUND If the matter of this paper be certain, you have mighty business in hand.

CORNWALL True or false, it hath made thee Earl of Gloucester. Seek out where thy father is, that he may be
20 ready for our apprehension.

---

184 *Child . . . came* (presumably a line from a ballad about the hero of the *Chanson de Roland*; child = a knight in training) **185–86** *His . . . man* (Edgar switches to a ballad about Jack the Giant Killer; word = motto, still = always)

III.5 Gloucester's house **3** *censured* criticized **3–4** *nature . . . loyalty* (the contrast is between familial and political bonds) **4** *something . . . me* I am almost afraid **7** *his* Gloucester's **8** *a . . . awork* a virtue incited to work **9** *himself* Gloucester (i.e., however wicked parricide is, Gloucester got what he deserved) **12** *approves* proves; *intelligent . . . of* spy on behalf of **20** *apprehension* arrest

EDMUND *[Aside]* If I find him comforting the king, it will stuff his suspicion more fully. – I will persever in my course of loyalty, though the conflict be sore between that and my blood. 21 24

CORNWALL I will lay trust upon thee, and thou shalt find a dearer father in my love. *Exeunt.*

*

❧ III.6 *Enter Kent [disguised] and Gloucester.*

GLOUCESTER Here is better than the open air; take it thankfully. I will piece out the comfort with what addition I can. I will not be long from you. 2

KENT All the power of his wits have given way to his impatience. The gods reward your kindness. 5

Exit [Gloucester].

Enter Lear, Edgar, and Fool.

EDGAR Frateretto calls me, and tells me Nero is an angler in the lake of darkness. Pray, innocent, and beware the foul fiend. 6

FOOL Prithee, nuncle, tell me whether a madman be a gentleman or a yeoman. 10

LEAR

A king, a king.

FOOL No, he's a yeoman that has a gentleman to his son; for he's a mad yeoman that sees his son a gentleman before him. 12 14

LEAR

To have a thousand with red burning spits
Come hissing in upon 'em –

---

21 *comforting* abetting **24** *blood* family ties

III.6 Within the hovel **2** *piece out* augment **5** *impatience* passion, rage **6** *Frateretto* (another devil from Harsnett's *Declaration*; see III.4.139); *Nero* (the diabolical Roman emperor, here condemned, following Chaucer's Monk's Tale, to fish in the lake of hell) **10** *yeoman* a landowner, but not a gentleman **12** *to* as **14** *before him* i.e., before he himself has been raised to the gentry

[EDGAR The foul fiend bites my back.
FOOL He's mad that trusts in the tameness of a wolf, a horse's health, a boy's love, or a whore's oath.
LEAR
It shall be done; I will arraign them straight.
[To Edgar]
Come, sit thou here, most learnèd justice.
[To the Fool]
Thou, sapient sir, sit here. Now, you she-foxes –
EDGAR Look, where he stands and glares. Want'st thou eyes at trial, madam?
Come o'er the burn, Bessy, to me.
FOOL Her boat hath a leak,
And she must not speak
Why she dares not come over to thee.
EDGAR The foul fiend haunts poor Tom in the voice of a nightingale. Hoppedance cries in Tom's belly for two white herring. Croak not, black angel; I have no food for thee.
KENT
How do you, sir? Stand you not so amazed.
Will you lie down and rest upon the cushions?
LEAR
I'll see their trial first. Bring in their evidence.
[To Edgar]
Thou, robèd man of justice, take thy place.
[To the Fool]
And thou, his yokefellow of equity,

---

20 *arraign . . . straight* put them on trial immediately **23–24** *Want'st . . . eyes* do you lack for spectators (?); are you blind (?) **25** *Come . . . me* (From a popular ballad; burn = stream. The fool's continuation is an obscene parody, punning on "burn" as the pain of venereal disease.) **26** *boat . . . leak* (both from the effects of the disease and because women are proverbially "leaky vessels") **30** *Hoppedance* (another devil from Harsnett) **31** *white* fresh; *Croak not* i.e., stop rumbling, belly **33** *amazed* bewildered **37** *yokefellow . . . equity* fellow judge

Bench by his side. *[To Kent]* You are o' th' commission; 38
Sit you too.

EDGAR Let us deal justly. *40*
Sleepest or wakest thou, jolly shepherd?
Thy sheep be in the corn; 42
And for one blast of thy minikin mouth 43
Thy sheep shall take no harm.
Purr, the cat is gray. 45

LEAR Arraign her first. 'Tis Goneril, I here take my oath before this honorable assembly, kicked the poor king her father.

FOOL Come hither, mistress. Is your name Goneril?

LEAR She cannot deny it. *50*

FOOL Cry you mercy, I took you for a joint stool. 51

LEAR
And here's another, whose warped looks proclaim
What store her heart is made on. Stop her there! 53
Arms, arms, sword, fire! Corruption in the place! 54
False justicer, why hast thou let her scape?]

EDGAR Bless thy five wits!

KENT
O pity! Sir, where is the patience now
That you so oft have boasted to retain?

EDGAR *[Aside]*
My tears begin to take his part so much
They mar my counterfeiting. *60*

LEAR
The little dogs and all, 61
Tray, Blanch, and Sweetheart – see, they bark at me.

---

38 *Bench* preside; *o' th' commission* i.e., presiding as a judge **42** *corn* wheat **43** *minikin* pretty, little **45** *Purr, the cat* (another Harsnett devil, here taking the form of a cat) **51** *I . . . joint stool* I beg your pardon, I mistook you for a stool – i.e., I didn't notice you; but the stool here is standing in for Goneril **53** *store* material; *on* of **54** *Corruption . . . place* i.e., there's bribery in the court **61** *The . . . all* even the lapdogs

EDGAR Tom will throw his head at them. Avaunt, you curs.
Be thy mouth or black or white,
Tooth that poisons if it bite;
Mastiff, greyhound, mongrel grim,
Hound or spaniel, brach or lym,
Or bobtail tike, or trundletail –
Tom will make him weep and wail;
For, with throwing thus my head,
Dogs leaped the hatch, and all are fled.
Do, de, de, de. Sessa! Come, march to wakes and fairs and market towns. Poor Tom, thy horn is dry.

LEAR Then let them anatomize Regan. See what breeds about her heart. Is there any cause in nature that makes these hard hearts? *[To Edgar]* You, sir, I entertain for one of my hundred; only I do not like the fashion of your garments. You will say they are Persian; but let them be changed.

KENT
Now, good my lord, lie here and rest awhile.

LEAR
Make no noise, make no noise; draw the curtains.
So, so. We'll go to supper i' th' morning.

FOOL And I'll go to bed at noon.

Enter Gloucester.

GLOUCESTER
Come hither, friend. Where is the king my master?

KENT
Here, sir, but trouble him not; his wits are gone.

---

63 *throw* shake; *Avaunt* get away **65** *or black* either black **68** *brach . . . lym* bitch or bloodhound **69** *bobtail . . . trundletail* short- or long-tailed mongrel **72** *hatch* lower half of a Dutch door **73** *Sessa!* stop! (French *cessez*); *wakes* festivals **74** *horn is dry* drinking horn is empty (i.e., "I've run out of steam") **75** *anatomize* dissect **77 s.d.** (or perhaps addressed to Kent, who has, ironically, been in Lear's service); *entertain* employ **79** *Persian* luxurious **82** *curtains* i.e., about an imaginary four-poster bed

GLOUCESTER
Good friend, I prithee take him in thy arms.
I have o'erheard a plot of death upon him. 88
There is a litter ready; lay him in't
And drive toward Dover, friend, where thou shalt meet *90*
Both welcome and protection. Take up thy master.
If thou shouldst dally half an hour, his life,
With thine and all that offer to defend him,
Stand in assurèd loss. Take up, take up, 94
And follow me, that will to some provision 95
Give thee quick conduct.
[KENT Oppressèd nature sleeps.
This rest might yet have balmed thy broken sinews,
Which, if convenience will not allow, 98
Stand in hard cure. 99
[To the Fool] Come, help to bear thy master.
Thou must not stay behind.] *100*
GLOUCESTER Come, come, away!
Exeunt [all but Edgar].
[EDGAR
When we our betters see bearing our woes, 101
We scarcely think our miseries our foes.
Who alone suffers suffers most i' th' mind,
Leaving free things and happy shows behind; 104
But then the mind much sufferance doth o'erskip
When grief hath mates, and bearing fellowship. 106
How light and portable my pain seems now, 107
When that which makes me bend makes the king bow.
He childed as I fatherèd. Tom, away. 109
Mark the high noises, and thyself bewray 110

---

88 *upon* against **94** *Stand . . . loss* will surely be lost **95–96** *to . . . conduct* will quickly lead you to provisions for the journey **98** *convenience* circumstances **99** *Stand . . . cure* will be hard to cure **101** *bearing . . . woes* enduring the same suffering as we do **104** *free* carefree; *shows* scenes **106** *bearing fellowship* endurance has company **107** *portable* bearable **109** *He* he is **110** *Mark . . . noises* follow the news of those in power; *bewray* reveal

111 When false opinion, whose wrong thoughts defile thee,
In thy just proof repeals and reconciles thee.
113 What will hap more tonight, safe scape the king!
Lurk, lurk.] *[Exit.]*

*

❧ **III.7** *Enter Cornwall, Regan, Goneril, Bastard [Edmund], and Servants.*

1 CORNWALL *[To Goneril]* Post speedily to my lord your husband; show him this letter. The army of France is landed. *[To Servants]* Seek out the traitor Gloucester.
[Exeunt some Servants.]

REGAN Hang him instantly.

GONERIL Pluck out his eyes.

CORNWALL Leave him to my displeasure. Edmund, keep
7 you our sister company. The revenges we are bound to take upon your traitorous father are not fit for your be-
9 holding. Advise the duke where you are going, to a
10 most festinate preparation. We are bound to the like.
11 Our posts shall be swift and intelligent betwixt us.
12 Farewell, dear sister; farewell, my Lord of Gloucester.
Enter Steward [Oswald].
How now? Where's the king?

OSWALD
My Lord of Gloucester hath conveyed him hence.
Some five or six and thirty of his knights,
16 Hot questrists after him, met him at gate;
Who, with some other of the lord's dependents,
Are gone with him toward Dover, where they boast
To have well-armèd friends.

111–12 *When . . . repeals* when proof of your innocence vindicates **113** *What . . . more* whatever more happens

III.7 Gloucester's house **1** *Post* ride **7** *sister* i.e., Goneril **9–10** *a . . . preparation* prepare quickly **10** *are . . . to* must do **11** *posts* messengers; *intelligent* informative **12** *my . . . Gloucester* (Edmund has been given his father's title) **16** *questrists* searchers

CORNWALL Get horses for your mistress. *Exit [Oswald].* 20

GONERIL
Farewell, sweet lord, and sister.

CORNWALL
Edmund, farewell.
[Exeunt Goneril and Edmund.]
Go seek the traitor Gloucester,
Pinion him like a thief, bring him before us. 23
[Exeunt other Servants.]
Though well we may not pass upon his life 24
Without the form of justice, yet our power
Shall do a court'sy to our wrath, which men 26
May blame, but not control.
Enter Gloucester and Servants.
Who's there, the traitor?

REGAN
Ingrateful fox, 'tis he.

CORNWALL
Bind fast his corky arms. 29

GLOUCESTER
What means your graces? Good my friends, consider 30
You are my guests. Do me no foul play, friends.

CORNWALL
Bind him, I say.
[Servants bind him.]

REGAN Hard, hard! O filthy traitor.

GLOUCESTER
Unmerciful lady as you are, I'm none.

CORNWALL
To this chair bind him. *[To Gloucester]* Villain, thou shalt find –
[Regan plucks Gloucester's beard.]

GLOUCESTER
By the kind gods, 'tis most ignobly done
To pluck me by the beard. 36

---

23 *Pinion him* tie him up **24** *pass* pass sentence **26** *do . . . to* defer to **29** *corky* dry, withered **36** *To . . . beard* (considered an extreme insult)

REGAN
37 So white, and such a traitor?
GLOUCESTER Naughty lady,
These hairs which thou dost ravish from my chin
39 Will quicken and accuse thee. I am your host.
40 With robber's hands my hospitable favors
41 You should not ruffle thus. What will you do?
CORNWALL
42 Come, sir, what letters had you late from France?
REGAN
43 Be simple-answered, for we know the truth.
CORNWALL
And what confederacy have you with the traitors
45 Late footed in the kingdom?
REGAN
To whose hands you have sent the lunatic king.
Speak.
GLOUCESTER
48 I have a letter guessingly set down,
Which came from one that's of a neutral heart,
50 And not from one opposed.
CORNWALL Cunning.
REGAN And false.
CORNWALL
Where hast thou sent the king?
GLOUCESTER
To Dover.
REGAN
53 Wherefore to Dover? Wast thou not charged at peril –
CORNWALL
Wherefore to Dover? Let him answer that.

---

37 *Naughty* evil 39 *quicken* come to life 40 *hospitable favors* welcoming face 41 *ruffle* tear at 42 *late* lately 43 *Be simple-answered* answer plainly 45 *Late footed* lately landed 48 *guessingly* speculatively 53 *charged at peril* ordered at peril of your life

GLOUCESTER
I am tied to th' stake, and I must stand the course. 55
REGAN
Wherefore to Dover?
GLOUCESTER
Because I would not see thy cruel nails
Pluck out his poor old eyes; nor thy fierce sister
In his anointed flesh stick boarish fangs. 59
The sea, with such a storm as his bare head *60*
In hell-black night endured, would have buoyed up 61
And quenched the stellèd fires. 62
Yet, poor old heart, he holp the heavens to rain. 63
If wolves had at thy gate howled that stern time,
Thou shouldst have said, "Good porter, turn the key." 65
All cruels else subscribe. But I shall see 66
The wingèd vengeance overtake such children. 67
CORNWALL
See't shalt thou never. Fellows, hold the chair.
Upon these eyes of thine I'll set my foot.
GLOUCESTER
He that will think to live till he be old, *70*
Give me some help. – O cruel! O you gods!
[Cornwall puts out Gloucester's eye.]
REGAN
One side will mock another. Th' other too.
CORNWALL
If you see vengeance –
FIRST SERVANT Hold your hand, my lord!
I have served you ever since I was a child;
But better service have I never done you
Than now to bid you hold.

---

55 *I am . . . course* (the image is from bearbaiting, in which the animal is tied to a stake and attacked by dogs) **59** *anointed* consecrated **61** *buoyed* swelled **62** *stellèd* stellar **63** *holp* helped **65** *turn the key* open the door **66** *All . . . subscribe* all other cruel creatures submit (to feelings of compassion) (?) **67** *wingèd vengeance* avenging Furies

REGAN How now, you dog?
FIRST SERVANT
If you did wear a beard upon your chin,
78 I'd shake it on this quarrel. What do you mean!
CORNWALL
79 My villain!
[Draw and fight.]
FIRST SERVANT
80 Nay, then, come on, and take the chance of anger.
REGAN
Give me thy sword. A peasant stand up thus?
[She takes a sword and runs at him behind;] kills him.
FIRST SERVANT
O, I am slain! My lord, you have one eye left
To see some mischief on him. O!
CORNWALL
Lest it see more, prevent it. Out, vile jelly.
[Puts out Gloucester's other eye.]
Where is thy luster now?
GLOUCESTER
All dark and comfortless. Where's my son Edmund?
Edmund, enkindle all the sparks of nature
88 To quit this horrid act.
REGAN Out, treacherous villain;
Thou call'st on him that hates thee. It was he
90 That made the overture of thy treasons to us;
Who is too good to pity thee.
GLOUCESTER
92 O my follies! Then Edgar was abused.
Kind gods, forgive me that, and prosper him.

---

78 *shake . . . quarrel* pluck it in this cause; *What . . . mean* i.e., how dare you **79** *villain* (the word retained some of its original meaning of serf or servant) **80** *chance . . . anger* risk of an angry fight **88** *quit* avenge **90** *made . . . of* revealed **92** *abused* wronged

REGAN

Go thrust him out at gates, and let him smell
His way to Dover. *Exit [a Servant] with Gloucester.* 95
How is't, my lord? How look you?

CORNWALL

I have received a hurt. Follow me, lady.
[To Servants]
Turn out that eyeless villain. Throw this slave
Upon the dunghill. Regan, I bleed apace.
Untimely comes this hurt. Give me your arm. *Exeunt.*

[SECOND SERVANT

I'll never care what wickedness I do, *100*
If this man come to good.

THIRD SERVANT If she live long,
And in the end meet the old course of death, 102
Women will all turn monsters.

SECOND SERVANT

Let's follow the old earl, and get the Bedlam
To lead him where he would. His roguish madness
Allows itself to anything. *[Exit.]*

THIRD SERVANT

Go thou. I'll fetch some flax and whites of eggs
To apply to his bleeding face. Now heaven help him.
Exit.]

*

~ IV.1 *Enter Edgar.*

EDGAR

Yet better thus, and known to be contemned, 1
Than still contemned and flattered. To be worst, 2
The lowest and most dejected thing of fortune,
Stands still in esperance, lives not in fear. 4

---

95 *How . . . you* how do you feel **102** *meet . . . death* die a natural death

IV.1 Open country **1** *contemned* despised **2** *still* always **4** *Stands . . . esperance* always has hope (because he has no fear of falling lower)

The lamentable change is from the best;
6 The worst returns to laughter. Welcome then,
Thou unsubstantial air that I embrace:
The wretch that thou hast blown unto the worst
9 Owes nothing to thy blasts.
Enter Gloucester and an Old Man.
But who comes here?
10 My father, poorly led? World, world, O world!
11 But that thy strange mutations make us hate thee,
12 Life would not yield to age. *[Stands aside.]*

OLD MAN *[To Gloucester]* O my good lord,
I have been your tenant, and your father's tenant,
These fourscore years.

GLOUCESTER
Away, get thee away. Good friend, be gone.
Thy comforts can do me no good at all;
Thee they may hurt.

OLD MAN You cannot see your way.

GLOUCESTER
I have no way, and therefore want no eyes;
I stumbled when I saw. Full oft 'tis seen
20 Our means secure us, and our mere defects
21 Prove our commodities. O dear son Edgar,
22 The food of thy abusèd father's wrath,
Might I but live to see thee in my touch
I'd say I had eyes again.

OLD MAN How now? Who's there?

EDGAR *[Aside]*
O gods! Who is't can say "I am at the worst"?
I am worse than e'er I was.

OLD MAN 'Tis poor mad Tom.

---

6 *returns to laughter* i.e., can only get better 9 *Owes nothing to* is not indebted to 11 *But* except 12 *yield to age* be reconciled to growing old 20 *Our . . . us* our prosperity makes us overconfident; *mere defects* utter deprivation 21 *commodities* advantages 22 *food* prey

EDGAR *[Aside]*
And worse I may be yet. The worst is not
So long as we can say "This is the worst."
OLD MAN Fellow, where goest?
GLOUCESTER Is it a beggarman? *30*
OLD MAN Madman and beggar too.
GLOUCESTER
He has some reason, else he could not beg. 32
I' th' last night's storm I such a fellow saw,
Which made me think a man a worm. My son
Came then into my mind, and yet my mind
Was then scarce friends with him. I have heard more since.
As flies to wanton boys are we to th' gods; 37
They kill us for their sport.
EDGAR *[Aside]* How should this be?
Bad is the trade that must play fool to sorrow, 39
Ang'ring itself and others. – Bless thee, master. *40*
GLOUCESTER
Is that the naked fellow?
OLD MAN Ay, my lord.
GLOUCESTER
Then prithee get thee gone. If for my sake
Thou wilt o'ertake us hence a mile or twain
I' th' way toward Dover, do it for ancient love; 44
And bring some covering for this naked soul,
Which I'll entreat to lead me.
OLD MAN Alack, sir, he is mad.
GLOUCESTER
'Tis the time's plague when madmen lead the blind. 48

---

32 *reason* sanity **37** *wanton* playful, irresponsible **39** *Bad . . . sorrow* playing the fool in the presence of grief is a bad business **44** *ancient love* our long relationship (as lord and tenant) **48** *time's plague* sickness of the times

Do as I bid thee, or rather do thy pleasure.
50 Above the rest, be gone.

OLD MAN

51 I'll bring him the best 'parel that I have,
52 Come on't what will. *Exit.*

GLOUCESTER

Sirrah naked fellow –

EDGAR

54 Poor Tom's acold. *[Aside]* I cannot daub it further.

GLOUCESTER

Come hither, fellow.

EDGAR *[Aside]*

And yet I must. – Bless thy sweet eyes, they bleed.

GLOUCESTER

Know'st thou the way to Dover?

EDGAR Both stile and gate, horseway and footpath. Poor
Tom hath been scared out of his good wits. Bless thee,
60 good man's son, from the foul fiend. [Five fiends have
been in poor Tom at once: of lust, as Obidicut; Hobbi-
didence, prince of dumbness; Mahu, of stealing; Modo,
63 of murder; Flibbertigibbet, of mopping and mowing,
who since possesses chambermaids and waiting women.
So, bless thee, master.]

GLOUCESTER

Here, take this purse, thou whom the heavens' plagues
67 Have humbled to all strokes. That I am wretched
Makes thee the happier. Heavens, deal so still!
69 Let the superfluous and lust-dieted man,
70 That slaves your ordinance, that will not see
Because he does not feel, feel your pow'r quickly;
So distribution should undo excess,
And each man have enough. Dost thou know Dover?

---

50 *Above . . . rest* above all **51** *'parel* apparel **52** *Come . . . will* whatever may come of it **54** *daub it* lay it on – i.e., act the part **63** *mopping . . . mowing* making faces **67** *humbled to* reduced to bearing meekly **69** *superfluous . . . man* man who has too much and feeds his desires **70** *slaves . . . ordinance* makes a slave of heaven's injunction (to give to the poor)

EDGAR Ay, master.
GLOUCESTER
There is a cliff, whose high and bending head 75
Looks fearfully in the confinèd deep. 76
Bring me but to the very brim of it,
And I'll repair the misery thou dost bear
With something rich about me. From that place
I shall no leading need. 80
EDGAR Give me thy arm.
Poor Tom shall lead thee. *Exeunt.*

*

❧ **IV.2** *Enter Goneril, Bastard [Edmund], and Steward [Oswald].*

GONERIL
Welcome, my lord. I marvel our mild husband
Not met us on the way. 2
[To Oswald] Now, where's your master?
OSWALD
Madam, within, but never man so changed.
I told him of the army that was landed:
He smiled at it. I told him you were coming:
His answer was, "The worse." Of Gloucester's treachery
And of the loyal service of his son
When I informed him, then he called me sot 8
And told me I had turned the wrong side out.
What most he should dislike seems pleasant to him; 10
What like, offensive.
GONERIL *[To Edmund]* Then shall you go no further.
It is the cowish terror of his spirit, 12
That dares not undertake. He'll not feel wrongs 13

---

75 *bending* overhanging 76 *in . . . deep* over the straits (of the English Channel) below

IV.2 Before Albany's castle 2 *Not* has not 8 *sot* fool 12 *cowish* cowardly 13 *undertake* commit himself to action 13–14 *He'll . . . answer* he'll ignore injuries that require him to retaliate

Which tie him to an answer. Our wishes on the way
15 May prove effects. Back, Edmund, to my brother.
16 Hasten his musters and conduct his pow'rs.
17 I must change names at home, and give the distaff
Into my husband's hands. This trusty servant
19 Shall pass between us. Ere long you are like to hear
20 (If you dare venture in your own behalf)
21 A mistress's command. Wear this. Spare speech.
[Gives a favor.]
Decline your head. This kiss, if it durst speak,
Would stretch thy spirits up into the air.
24 Conceive, and fare thee well.

EDMUND

25 Yours in the ranks of death. *Exit.*

GONERIL My most dear Gloucester.
O, the difference of man and man:
To thee a woman's services are due;
28 My fool usurps my body.

OSWALD Madam, here comes my lord.

[Exit.]

Enter Albany.

GONERIL

30 I have been worth the whistle.

ALBANY O Goneril,
You are not worth the dust which the rude wind
Blows in your face. [I fear your disposition:
33 That nature which contemns its origin
34 Cannot be bordered certain in itself.

---

15 *prove effects* be fulfilled; *brother* brother-in-law, Cornwall **16** *his musters* the muster of his troops; *conduct . . . pow'rs* guide his forces **17** *names* roles **17–18** *give . . . hands* give my husband the housewife's spinning staff **19** *like* likely **21** *Wear this* (Goneril gives Edmund a lover's token, such as a handkerchief or a glove) **24** *Conceive* understand me **25** *in the ranks of* even up to **28** *My . . . body* i.e., my idiot husband wrongfully possesses me **30** *I . . . whistle* "I used to be worth welcoming home" (alluding to the proverbial poor dog who is "not worth the whistle") **33** *contemns* despises **34** *Cannot . . . certain* can have no secure boundaries

She that herself will sliver and disbranch 35
From her material sap, perforce must wither
And come to deadly use. 37

GONERIL

No more; the text is foolish.

ALBANY

Wisdom and goodness to the vile seem vile;
Filths savor but themselves. What have you done? *40*
Tigers not daughters, what have you performed?
A father, and a gracious agèd man,
Whose reverence even the head-lugged bear would lick, 43
Most barbarous, most degenerate, have you madded. 44
Could my good brother suffer you to do it? 45
A man, a prince, by him so benefited!
If that the heavens do not their visible spirits
Send quickly down to tame these vile offenses,
It will come,
Humanity must perforce prey on itself, *50*
Like monsters of the deep.] 51

GONERIL Milk-livered man,
That bear'st a cheek for blows, a head for wrongs; 52
Who hast not in thy brows an eye discerning 53
Thine honor from thy suffering; [that not know'st
Fools do those villains pity who are punished 55
Ere they have done their mischief. Where's thy drum? 56
France spreads his banners in our noiseless land, 57
With plumèd helm thy state begins to threat, 58

---

35 *sliver and disbranch* cut herself off and split away **37** *deadly use* destructiveness **43** *head-lugged* dragged by a chain around its neck (and thus ill-tempered) **44** *madded* driven mad **45** *brother* brother-in-law **51** *Milk-livered* cowardly **52** *for* fit for **53–54** *discerning . . . suffering* that can distinguish what affects your honor (and thus must be resisted) from what must be endured **55** *Fools* i.e., only fools **56** *drum* i.e., why are you not mustering your army? **57** *France* the King of France; *noiseless* silent (without the sound of military drums) **58** *thy . . . threat* begins to threaten thy state (a famous crux, much emended)

59 Whilst thou, a moral fool, sits still and cries
60 "Alack, why does he so?"]

ALBANY See thyself, devil:
61 Proper deformity seems not in the fiend
62 So horrid as in woman.

GONERIL O vain fool!

[ALBANY
63 Thou changèd and self-covered thing, for shame
64 Bemonster not thy feature. Were't my fitness
65 To let these hands obey my blood,
They are apt enough to dislocate and tear
67 Thy flesh and bones. Howe'er thou art a fiend,
A woman's shape doth shield thee.

GONERIL
69 Marry, your manhood – mew!]

Enter a Messenger.

70 [ALBANY What news?]

MESSENGER
O, my good lord, the Duke of Cornwall's dead,
Slain by his servant, going to put out
The other eye of Gloucester.

ALBANY Gloucester's eyes?

MESSENGER
74 A servant that he bred, thrilled with remorse,
Opposed against the act, bending his sword
To his great master; who, thereat enraged,
Flew on him, and amongst them felled him dead;
But not without that harmful stroke which since
Hath plucked him after.

ALBANY This shows you are above,
80 You justicers, that these our nether crimes

---

59 *moral* moralizing **61** *Proper . . . not* a deformed nature does not appear **62** *vain* silly, worthless **63** *self-covered* hiding your true nature **64** *Were't . . . fitness* if it were appropriate for me **65** *blood* passion **67** *Howe'er* although **69** *Marry . . . mew* lock up your manhood (*Marry* = an interjection, originally an oath on the name of the Virgin Mary) **74** *thrilled . . . remorse* overwhelmed with pity **80** *justicers* (heavenly) judges

So speedily can venge. But, O poor Gloucester,
Lost he his other eye?

MESSENGER Both, both, my lord.
This letter, madam, craves a speedy answer.
'Tis from your sister.

GONERIL *[Aside]* One way I like this well;
But being widow, and my Gloucester with her, 85
May all the building in my fancy pluck 86
Upon my hateful life. Another way 87
The news is not so tart. – I'll read, and answer. *[Exit.]* 88

ALBANY
Where was his son when they did take his eyes?

MESSENGER
Come with my lady hither. *90*

ALBANY He is not here.

MESSENGER
No, my good lord; I met him back again. 91

ALBANY
Knows he the wickedness?

MESSENGER
Ay, my good lord. 'Twas he informed against him,
And quit the house on purpose, that their punishment
Might have the freer course.

ALBANY Gloucester, I live
To thank thee for the love thou show'dst the king,
And to revenge thine eyes. Come hither, friend.
Tell me what more thou know'st. *Exeunt.*

*

☙ IV.3 *[Enter Kent [disguised] and a Gentleman.*

KENT Why the King of France is so suddenly gone back
know you no reason?

---

85 *being* she being **86** *all . . . pluck* pull down my dream castles **87** *Another way* i.e., returning to the *One way* of l. 84 **88** *tart* distasteful **91** *back* returning

IV.3 Near Dover

3 GENTLEMAN Something he left imperfect in the state,
4 which since his coming forth is thought of, which imports to the kingdom so much fear and danger that his personal return was most required and necessary.

KENT
Who hath he left behind him general?

GENTLEMAN The Marshal of France, Monsieur La Far.

KENT Did your letters pierce the queen to any demon-
10 stration of grief?

GENTLEMAN
Ay, sir. She took them, read them in my presence,
And now and then an ample tear trilled down
Her delicate cheek. It seemed she was a queen
Over her passion, who, most rebel-like,
Sought to be king o'er her.

KENT O, then it moved her?

GENTLEMAN
Not to a rage. Patience and sorrow strove
17 Who should express her goodliest. You have seen
Sunshine and rain at once – her smiles and tears
19 Were like, a better way: those happy smilets
20 That played on her ripe lip seemed not to know
What guests were in her eyes, which parted thence
As pearls from diamonds dropped. In brief,
23 Sorrow would be a rarity most belovèd,
24 If all could so become it.

KENT Made she no verbal question?

GENTLEMAN
Faith, once or twice she heaved the name of father
Pantingly forth, as if it pressed her heart;
Cried "Sisters, sisters, shame of ladies, sisters!
Kent, father, sisters? What, i' th' storm, i' th' night?

---

3 *imperfect* incomplete 4–5 *imports to* threatens 17 *Who . . . goodliest* which should best express her feelings 19 *like . . . way* like that, only better 23 *rarity* jewel 24 *all . . . it* everyone wore it so well

Let pity not be believed!" There she shook 30
The holy water from her heavenly eyes,
And clamor moistened; then away she started 32
To deal with grief alone.

KENT It is the stars,
The stars above us govern our conditions;
Else one self mate and make could not beget 35
Such different issues. You spoke not with her since? 36

GENTLEMAN No.

KENT
Was this before the king returned?

GENTLEMAN No, since.

KENT
Well, sir, the poor distressèd Lear's i' th' town;
Who sometime, in his better tune, remembers 40
What we are come about, and by no means
Will yield to see his daughter.

GENTLEMAN Why, good sir?

KENT
A sovereign shame so elbows him; his own unkindness,
That stripped her from his benediction, turned her
To foreign casualties, gave her dear rights 45
To his dog-hearted daughters – these things sting
His mind so venomously that burning shame
Detains him from Cordelia.

GENTLEMAN Alack, poor gentleman.

KENT
Of Albany's and Cornwall's powers you heard not? 50

GENTLEMAN 'Tis so; they are afoot.

---

30 *Let . . . believed* never trust in pity; or, how can pity be believed to exist? 32 *clamor moistened* moistened her grief with tears 35 *one . . . make* one married couple (*mate* and *make* both mean *spouse*) 36 *issues* offspring 40 *better tune* more rational state 45 *casualties* dangers; *dear* valuable 50 *powers* forces

KENT

Well, sir, I'll bring you to our master Lear
And leave you to attend him. Some dear cause
Will in concealment wrap me up awhile.
When I am known aright, you shall not grieve
Lending me this acquaintance. I pray you go
Along with me. *Exeunt.*]

*

❧ IV.4 *Enter, with Drum and Colors, Cordelia, Gentlemen, [Doctor], and Soldiers.*

CORDELIA

Alack, 'tis he! Why, he was met even now
As mad as the vexed sea, singing aloud,
Crowned with rank fumiter and furrow weeds,
With hardocks, hemlock, nettles, cuckooflow'rs,
Darnel, and all the idle weeds that grow
In our sustaining corn. A century send forth!
Search every acre in the high-grown field
And bring him to our eye. *[Exit an Officer.]*
What can man's wisdom
In the restoring his bereavèd sense?
He that helps him take all my outward worth.

DOCTOR

There is means, madam.
Our foster nurse of nature is repose,
The which he lacks. That to provoke in him
Are many simples operative, whose power
Will close the eye of anguish.

---

53 *dear* important 55 *grieve* regret

IV.4 The French camp near Dover **s.d.** *Drum and Colors* drummer and standard-bearer 3 *fumiter* fumitory; this, and the following, are all field weeds 5 *idle* useless, uncultivated 6 *sustaining corn* life-sustaining wheat; *century* troop of one hundred soldiers 8 *What . . . wisdom* whatever man's wisdom can do 10 *outward worth* material possessions 12 *Our . . . nature* what naturally cares for us 13 *provoke* induce 14 *simples operative* herbal remedies

CORDELIA All blessed secrets,
All you unpublished virtues of the earth, 16
Spring with my tears; be aidant and remediate 17
In the good man's distress. Seek, seek for him,
Lest his ungoverned rage dissolve the life
That wants the means to lead it. 20

Enter Messenger.

MESSENGER News, madam.
The British pow'rs are marching hitherward.

CORDELIA
'Tis known before. Our preparation stands
In expectation of them. O dear father,
It is thy business that I go about.
Therefore great France 25
My mourning, and importuned tears hath pitied. 26
No blown ambition doth our arms incite, 27
But love, dear love, and our aged father's right.
Soon may I hear and see him! *Exeunt.*

*

❧ IV.5 *Enter Regan and Steward [Oswald].*

REGAN
But are my brother's pow'rs set forth? 1

OSWALD Ay, madam.

REGAN
Himself in person there?

OSWALD
Madam, with much ado. 4
Your sister is the better soldier.

REGAN
Lord Edmund spake not with your lord at home?

OSWALD No, madam.

---

16 *unpublished virtues* secret powers 17 *be . . . remediate* aid and heal 20 *wants* lacks 25 *France* the King of France 26 *importuned* importuning 27 *blown* presumptuous

IV.5 Gloucester's house 1 *brother's pow'rs* Albany's forces 4 *ado* difficulty

REGAN
What might import my sister's letter to him?
OSWALD I know not, lady.
REGAN
10 Faith, he is posted hence on serious matter.
It was great ignorance, Gloucester's eyes being out,
To let him live. Where he arrives he moves
All hearts against us. Edmund, I think, is gone,
In pity of his misery, to dispatch
15 His nighted life; moreover, to descry
The strength o' th' enemy.
OSWALD
I must needs after him, madam, with my letter.
REGAN
Our troops set forth tomorrow. Stay with us.
The ways are dangerous.
OSWALD I may not, madam.
20 My lady charged my duty in this business.
REGAN
Why should she write to Edmund? Might not you
22 Transport her purposes by word? Belike,
Some things – I know not what. I'll love thee much,
Let me unseal the letter.
OSWALD Madam, I had rather –
REGAN
I know your lady does not love her husband,
27 I am sure of that; and at her late being here
28 She gave strange eliads and most speaking looks
29 To noble Edmund. I know you are of her bosom.
30 OSWALD I, madam?
REGAN
31 I speak in understanding – y'are, I know't.

---

10 *is posted hence* rushed away from here **15** *nighted* both benighted and blind; *descry* spy out **20** *charged* strictly commanded **22** *Belike* perhaps **27** *late* recently **28** *eliads* amorous glances **29** *of . . . bosom* in her confidence, with a sexual overtone **31** *understanding* certain knowledge

Therefore I do advise you take this note: 32
My lord is dead; Edmund and I have talked,
And more convenient is he for my hand 34
Than for your lady's. You may gather more. 35
If you do find him, pray you give him this; 36
And when your mistress hears thus much from you,
I pray desire her call her wisdom to her. 38
So fare you well.
If you do chance to hear of that blind traitor, 40
Preferment falls on him that cuts him off. 41

OSWALD
Would I could meet him, madam! I should show
What party I do follow.

REGAN Fare thee well. *Exeunt.*

*

☙ IV.6 *Enter Gloucester and Edgar.*

GLOUCESTER
When shall I come to th' top of that same hill?

EDGAR
You do climb up it now. Look how we labor.

GLOUCESTER
Methinks the ground is even.

EDGAR Horrible steep.
Hark, do you hear the sea?

GLOUCESTER No, truly.

EDGAR
Why, then, your other senses grow imperfect
By your eyes' anguish.

---

32 *take . . . note* take note of this 34 *convenient* appropriate 35 *gather more* infer more (from what I say) 36 *this* (Perhaps a token; perhaps a letter: Edgar finds only Goneril's letter in Oswald's pockets in IV.6.262, but Oswald, dying, speaks of "letters," so perhaps Edgar misses one. "Letters," on the other hand, could be singular.) 38 *wisdom to her* back to reason 41 *cuts him off* cuts short his life

IV.6 Open country near Dover

GLOUCESTER So may it be indeed.
Methinks thy voice is altered, and thou speak'st
In better phrase and matter than thou didst.
EDGAR
You're much deceived. In nothing am I changed
10 But in my garments.
GLOUCESTER Methinks you're better spoken.
EDGAR
Come on, sir; here's the place. Stand still. How fearful
And dizzy 'tis to cast one's eyes so low!
13 The crows and choughs that wing the midway air
14 Show scarce so gross as beetles. Halfway down
15 Hangs one that gathers samphire – dreadful trade;
Methinks he seems no bigger than his head.
The fishermen that walk upon the beach
18 Appear like mice; and yond tall anchoring bark,
19 Diminished to her cock; her cock, a buoy
20 Almost too small for sight. The murmuring surge
21 That on th' unnumb'red idle pebble chafes
Cannot be heard so high. I'll look no more,
Lest my brain turn, and the deficient sight
24 Topple down headlong.
GLOUCESTER Set me where you stand.
EDGAR
Give me your hand. You are now within a foot
Of th' extreme verge. For all beneath the moon
27 Would I not leap upright.
GLOUCESTER Let go my hand.
Here, friend, 's another purse; in it a jewel
Well worth a poor man's taking. Fairies and gods

---

13 *choughs* jackdaws; pronounced "chuffs" **14** *Show* appear; *gross* large **15** *samphire* Saint Peter's herb (used in pickling; it grows on steep cliffs, hence the danger in gathering it) **18** *bark* ship **19** *cock* dinghy **21** *unnumb'red . . . pebble* barren reach of innumerable pebbles **24** *Topple* topple me **27** *leap upright* jump upward (to jump forward would reveal to Gloucester that he is not on the edge of a cliff)

Prosper it with thee. Go thou further off; 30
Bid me farewell, and let me hear thee going.

EDGAR
Now fare ye well, good sir.

GLOUCESTER With all my heart.

EDGAR *[Aside]*
Why I do trifle thus with his despair
Is done to cure it.

GLOUCESTER O you mighty gods!
[He kneels.]
This world I do renounce, and in your sights
Shake patiently my great affliction off.
If I could bear it longer and not fall
To quarrel with your great opposeless wills,
My snuff and loathèd part of nature should 39
Burn itself out. If Edgar live, O bless him! *40*
Now, fellow, fare thee well.
[He falls forward and swoons.]

EDGAR Gone, sir – farewell.
And yet I know not how conceit may rob 42
The treasury of life when life itself
Yields to the theft. Had he been where he thought, 44
By this had thought been past. Alive or dead? 45
Ho you, sir! Friend! Hear you, sir? Speak!
Thus might he pass indeed. Yet he revives. 47
What are you, sir?

GLOUCESTER Away, and let me die.

EDGAR
Hadst thou been aught but gossamer, feathers, air, 49
So many fathom down precipitating, *50*
Thou'dst shivered like an egg; but thou dost breathe, 51

---

30 *Prosper* increase 39 *snuff* burnt-out candle end; *loathèd . . . nature* despised remnant of life 42 *conceit* illusion, imagination 44 *Yields to* accedes to, welcomes 45 *this* this time 47 *pass indeed* really die 49 *aught* anything 51 *shivered* shattered

Hast heavy substance, bleed'st not, speak'st, art sound.
53 Ten masts at each make not the altitude
Which thou hast perpendicularly fell.
Thy life's a miracle. Speak yet again.

GLOUCESTER
But have I fall'n, or no?

EDGAR
57 From the dread summit of this chalky bourn.
58 Look up aheight. The shrill-gorged lark so far
Cannot be seen or heard. Do but look up.

GLOUCESTER
60 Alack, I have no eyes.
61 Is wretchedness deprived that benefit
To end itself by death? 'Twas yet some comfort
63 When misery could beguile the tyrant's rage
And frustrate his proud will.

EDGAR Give me your arm.
Up – so. How is't? Feel you your legs? You stand.

GLOUCESTER
Too well, too well.

EDGAR This is above all strangeness.
Upon the crown o' th' cliff what thing was that
Which parted from you?

GLOUCESTER A poor unfortunate beggar.

EDGAR
As I stood here below, methought his eyes
70 Were two full moons; he had a thousand noses,
71 Horns whelked and waved like the enridgèd sea.
72 It was some fiend. Therefore, thou happy father,
73 Think that the clearest gods, who make them honors
Of men's impossibilities, have preservèd thee.

---

53 *at each* placed end to end 57 *chalky bourn* chalk cliff, the White Cliffs of Dover 58 *shrill-gorged* shrill-voiced 61 *deprived* denied 63 *beguile* cheat 71 *whelked* twisted 72 *happy father* lucky old man 73 *clearest* wisest, most glorious 73–74 *who . . . impossibilities* whose glory consists in performing miracles

GLOUCESTER
I do remember now. Henceforth I'll bear
Affliction till it do cry out itself
"Enough, enough," and die. That thing you speak of,
I took it for a man. Often 'twould say
"The fiend, the fiend" – he led me to that place.

EDGAR
Bear free and patient thoughts. *80*
Enter Lear [mad, bedecked with weeds].
But who comes here?
The safer sense will ne'er accommodate 81
His master thus.

LEAR No, they cannot touch me for coining; I am the 83
king himself.

EDGAR
O thou side-piercing sight!

LEAR Nature's above art in that respect. There's your 86
press money. That fellow handles his bow like a crow- 87
keeper. Draw me a clothier's yard. Look, look, a mouse! 88
Peace, peace; this piece of toasted cheese will do't. 89
There's my gauntlet; I'll prove it on a giant. Bring up 90
the brown bills. O, well flown, bird. I' th' clout, i' th' 91
clout – hewgh! Give the word. 92

EDGAR Sweet marjoram.

LEAR Pass.

GLOUCESTER I know that voice.

---

81 *The . . . sense* a sane mind; *accommodate* array **83** *touch* arrest; *coining* counterfeiting (because minting money was a royal prerogative) **86** *Nature . . . respect* i.e., kings are born, not made **87** *press money* payment for volunteering or being drafted to fight (Lear is conscripting an imaginary army) **87–88** *crowkeeper* scarecrow **88** *Draw . . . yard* draw the bow out fully (a clothier's yard, 37 inches, was the length of an arrow) **89** *do't* catch the mouse **90** *gauntlet* armored glove (thrown down as a challenge); *prove it on* uphold my cause against **91** *brown bills* pike carriers (Lear continues to assemble his army); *bird* arrow; *clout* bull's-eye **92** *word* password

LEAR Ha! Goneril with a white beard? They flattered me
97 like a dog, and told me I had the white hairs in my
beard ere the black ones were there. To say "ay" and
99 "no" to everything that I said! "Ay" and "no" too was no
100 good divinity. When the rain came to wet me once, and
the wind to make me chatter; when the thunder would
102 not peace at my bidding; there I found 'em, there I
smelt 'em out. Go to, they are not men o' their words.
They told me I was everything. 'Tis a lie – I am not
105 ague-proof.

GLOUCESTER

106 The trick of that voice I do well remember.
Is't not the king?

LEAR Ay, every inch a king.
When I do stare, see how the subject quakes.
109 I pardon that man's life. What was thy cause?
110 Adultery?
Thou shalt not die. Die for adultery? No.
The wren goes to't, and the small gilded fly
Does lecher in my sight.
Let copulation thrive; for Gloucester's bastard son
Was kinder to his father than my daughters
116 Got 'tween the lawful sheets.
117 To't, luxury, pell-mell, for I lack soldiers.
Behold yond simp'ring dame,
119 Whose face between her forks presages snow,
120 That minces virtue, and does shake the head
To hear of pleasure's name.
122 The fitchew nor the soilèd horse goes to't
With a more riotous appetite.

---

97 *like a dog* as a dog does – i.e., they fawned on me **97–98** *the . . . beard* i.e., the wisdom of age **99–100** *no . . . divinity* bad theology **102** *found 'em* found them out **105** *ague-proof* immune to fever **106** *trick* special quality **109** *cause* offense **116** *Got* begotten **117** *luxury* lechery **119** *face . . . forks* (both her face between the combs that hold her hair in place, and her genitals between her forked legs); *snow* sexual coldness, frigidity **120** *minces* affects **122** *fitchew* both polecat and prostitute; *soilèd* pastured, well-fed

Down from the waist they are centaurs, 124
Though women all above.
But to the girdle do the gods inherit, 126
Beneath is all the fiend's.
There's hell, there's darkness, there is the sulphurous pit; burning, scalding, stench, consumption. Fie, fie, fie! pah, pah! Give me an ounce of civet; good apothecary, sweeten my imagination! There's money for thee. 130

GLOUCESTER O, let me kiss that hand.

LEAR Let me wipe it first; it smells of mortality.

GLOUCESTER
O ruined piece of nature; this great world 134
Shall so wear out to nought. Dost thou know me? 135

LEAR I remember thine eyes well enough. Dost thou squiny at me? No, do thy worst, blind Cupid; I'll not love. Read thou this challenge; mark but the penning of it. 137

GLOUCESTER
Were all thy letters suns, I could not see. *140*

EDGAR *[Aside]*
I would not take this from report – it is, 141
And my heart breaks at it.

LEAR Read.

GLOUCESTER What, with the case of eyes? 144

LEAR O, ho, are you there with me? No eyes in your head, nor no money in your purse? Your eyes are in a heavy case, your purse in a light; yet you see how this world goes. 145 147

GLOUCESTER I see it feelingly.

---

124 *centaurs* (the classical centaurs were men to the waist and horses below, and were notoriously lustful) 126 *But . . . girdle* only down to the waist; *inherit* possess 130 *civet* perfume 134 *piece* masterpiece 135 *so . . . nought* decay to nothing in the same way 137 *squiny* squint 141 *take* believe; *is* is actually happening 144 *case* sockets 145 *are . . . me* is that what you mean (with an overtone of "Are we both blind?") 147 *heavy case* sad situation

150 LEAR What, art mad? A man may see how this world
goes with no eyes. Look with thine ears. See how yond
152 justice rails upon yond simple thief. Hark in thine ear:
153 change places and, handy-dandy, which is the justice,
which is the thief? Thou hast seen a farmer's dog bark at
a beggar?

GLOUCESTER Ay, sir.

157 LEAR And the creature run from the cur. There thou
might'st behold the great image of authority – a dog's
159 obeyed in office.
160 Thou rascal beadle, hold thy bloody hand!
Why dost thou lash that whore? Strip thy own back.
162 Thou hotly lusts to use her in that kind
163 For which thou whip'st her. The usurer hangs the coz-
ener.
Through tattered clothes small vices do appear;
165 Robes and furred gowns hide all. Plate sin with gold,
And the strong lance of justice hurtless breaks;
Arm it in rags, a pygmy's straw does pierce it.
168 None does offend, none – I say none! I'll able 'em.
169 Take that of me, my friend, who have the power
170 To seal th' accuser's lips. Get thee glass eyes
171 And, like a scurvy politician, seem
To see the things thou dost not. Now, now, now, now!
Pull off my boots. Harder, harder! So.

EDGAR

174 O, matter and impertinency mixed;
Reason in madness.

---

152 *simple* mere **153** *handy-dandy* the child's game "choose a hand" **157** *creature* man **159** *in office* in a position of power **160** *beadle* church constable **162** *kind* way **163** *usurer . . . cozener* i.e., the big thief hangs the little one; *usurer* = moneylender, *cozener* = cheat **165** *Plate . . . gold* cover sin in golden armor **168** *able 'em* vouch for their innocence **169** *Take . . . me* i.e., I pardon you too **170** *glass eyes* eyeglasses **171** *scurvy politician* vile Machiavel **174** *matter . . . impertinency* sense and nonsense

LEAR
If thou wilt weep my fortunes, take my eyes.
I know thee well enough; thy name is Gloucester.
Thou must be patient. We came crying hither;
Thou know'st, the first time that we smell the air
We wawl and cry. I will preach to thee. Mark. *180*
GLOUCESTER Alack, alack the day.
LEAR
When we are born, we cry that we are come
To this great stage of fools. – This' a good block. 183
It were a delicate stratagem to shoe 184
A troop of horse with felt. I'll put't in proof,
And when I have stol'n upon these son-in-laws,
Then kill, kill, kill, kill, kill, kill!
Enter a Gentleman [with Attendants].
GENTLEMAN
O, here he is! Lay hand upon him. – Sir,
Your most dear daughter –
LEAR
No rescue? What, a prisoner? I am even *190*
The natural fool of fortune. Use me well; 191
You shall have ransom. Let me have surgeons;
I am cut to th' brains.
GENTLEMAN You shall have anything.
LEAR
No seconds? All myself? 194
Why, this would make a man a man of salt, 195
To use his eyes for garden waterpots, 196
[Ay, and laying autumn's dust.] I will die bravely, 197

---

183 *This'* this is; *block* felt hat (either the hat decked with weeds, which he removes to begin his sermon, or an imaginary hat suggested by the crown of weeds) **184** *delicate* subtle **184–85** *shoe . . . felt* (and thus enable it to approach silently) **191** *natural fool* born plaything; *Use* treat **194** *seconds* supporters **195** *salt* tears **196** *waterpots* watering cans **197** *die* (with a quibble on the sexual sense, have an orgasm); *bravely* both courageously and handsomely

198 Like a smug bridegroom. What, I will be jovial!
Come, come, I am a king; masters, know you that?

GENTLEMAN

200 You are a royal one, and we obey you.

201 LEAR Then there's life in't. Come, an you get it, you shall
202 get it by running. Sa, sa, sa, sa!

Exit [running, followed by Attendants].

GENTLEMAN

A sight most pitiful in the meanest wretch,
Past speaking of in a king. Thou hast one daughter
205 Who redeems nature from the general curse
Which twain have brought her to.

EDGAR

207 Hail, gentle sir.

GENTLEMAN Sir, speed you. What's your will?

EDGAR

208 Do you hear aught, sir, of a battle toward?

GENTLEMAN

209 Most sure and vulgar. Every one hears that
210 Which can distinguish sound.

EDGAR But, by your favor,
How near's the other army?

GENTLEMAN

Near and on speedy foot. The main descry
213 Stands on the hourly thought.

EDGAR I thank you, sir. That's all.

GENTLEMAN

215 Though that the queen on special cause is here,
Her army is moved on.

---

198 *smug* neat; satisfied **201** *there's . . . in't* i.e., there's still hope; *an* if **202** *sa* a hunting cry **205–6** *general . . . to* the universal disruption caused by your other two daughters (but also the original sin caused by the filial ingratitude of the original pair, Adam and Eve) **207** *gentle* noble; *speed* God prosper **208** *toward* impending **209** *vulgar* common knowledge **210** *Which* who **213** *the . . . thought* the sight of the main body is expected hourly **215** *Though that* however; *on . . . cause* for a particular reason

EDGAR I thank you, sir. *Exit [Gentleman].*

GLOUCESTER

You ever-gentle gods, take my breath from me;
Let not my worser spirit tempt me again 218
To die before you please. 219

EDGAR Well pray you, father.

GLOUCESTER

Now, good sir, what are you? *220*

EDGAR

A most poor man, made tame to fortune's blows, 221
Who, by the art of known and feeling sorrows, 222
Am pregnant to good pity. Give me your hand; 223
I'll lead you to some biding. 224

GLOUCESTER Hearty thanks.

The bounty and the benison of heaven 225
To boot, and boot. 226

Enter Steward [Oswald].

OSWALD A proclaimed prize! Most happy;
That eyeless head of thine was first framed flesh 227
To raise my fortunes. Thou old unhappy traitor,
Briefly thyself remember. The sword is out 229
That must destroy thee. *230*

GLOUCESTER Now let thy friendly hand
Put strength enough to't.

[Edgar interposes.]

OSWALD Wherefore, bold peasant,
Dar'st thou support a published traitor? Hence, 232
Lest that th' infection of his fortune take
Like hold on thee. Let go his arm.

---

218 *worser spirit* "bad side" **219** *father* old man **221** *tame* submissive **222** *art . . . sorrows* lesson of sorrows experienced and deeply felt **223** *pregnant* prone **224** *biding* dwelling **225–26** *bounty . . . boot* may it bring you the bounty and blessing of heaven, and a reward in addition **226** *proclaimed prize* criminal with a price on his head; *happy* lucky **227** *framed flesh* made human **229** *thyself remember* i.e., remember your sins and pray **232** *published* proclaimed

EDGAR
235 Chill not let go, zir, without vurther 'casion.
OSWALD
Let go, slave, or thou diest.
237 EDGAR Good gentleman, go your gait, and let poor voke
238 pass. An chud ha' bin zwaggered out of my life, 'twould
not ha' bin zo long as 'tis by a vortnight. Nay, come not
240 near th' old man. Keep out, che vore ye, or Ise try
241 whether your costard or my ballow be the harder. Chill
be plain with you.
OSWALD Out, dunghill!
[They fight.]
244 EDGAR Chill pick your teeth, zir. Come. No matter vor
245 your foins.
[Oswald falls.]
OSWALD
Slave, thou hast slain me. Villain, take my purse.
If ever thou wilt thrive, bury my body,
248 And give the letters which thou find'st about me
To Edmund Earl of Gloucester. Seek him out
250 Upon the English party. O, untimely death!
Death!
[He dies.]
EDGAR
I know thee well. A serviceable villain,
As duteous to the vices of thy mistress
As badness would desire.
GLOUCESTER What, is he dead?

---

235 *Chill* I'll (Edgar adopts a west country dialect); *'casion* occasion, cause **237** *go your gait* be on your way **238** *An . . . zwaggered* if I could have been bullied **240** *che vore ye* I warn you **241** *your . . . ballow* your head or my cudgel **244** *pick . . . teeth* i.e., with my club **245** *foins* sword thrusts **248** *letters* (Oswald has a letter for Edmund from Goneril; if he has indeed been given one by Regan, too, as is implied at IV.5.36, Edgar fails to find it. But "letters" may be singular – the letters that together compose one letter – as at I.5.1) **250** *Upon* among

EDGAR

Sit you down, father; rest you.
Let's see these pockets; the letters that he speaks of
May be my friends. He's dead; I am only sorry
He had no other deathsman. Let us see.
Leave, gentle wax and manners: blame us not 259
To know our enemies' minds. We rip their hearts; 260
Their papers is more lawful. 261
Reads the letter.
"Let our reciprocal vows be remembered. You have
many opportunities to cut him off. If your will want 263
not, time and place will be fruitfully offered. There is 264
nothing done, if he return the conqueror. Then am I the 265
prisoner, and his bed my jail; from the loathed warmth
whereof deliver me, and supply the place for your labor. 267
"Your (wife, so I would say) affectionate servant,
"Goneril."
O indistinguished space of woman's will – 270
A plot upon her virtuous husband's life,
And the exchange my brother! – Here in the sands
Thee I'll rake up, the post unsanctified 273
Of murderous lechers; and in the mature time 274
With this ungracious paper strike the sight
Of the death-practiced duke. For him 'tis well 276
That of thy death and business I can tell. 277

GLOUCESTER

The king is mad. How stiff is my vile sense, 278

---

259 *Leave . . . wax* by your leave, kind seal **261** *Their* to rip their **263** *him* Albany **263–64** *If . . . not* if you do not lack the will **264** *fruitfully* i.e., promising success **265** *done* accomplished **267** *supply* fill **270** *indistinguished* unlimited **273** *rake up* cover over; *post unsanctified* unholy messenger **274** *in . . . time* when the time is ripe **276** *death-practiced* whose death is plotted **277** (None of the original texts makes any provision for the removal of Oswald's body. Editors since the eighteenth century have had Edgar exit here dragging it offstage, and then return six lines later. The very awkward alternative is for him to remove it while he is also leading Gloucester offstage.) **278** *How . . . sense* how obstinate is my hateful consciousness

That I stand up, and have ingenious feeling
Of my huge sorrows! Better I were distract;
So should my thoughts be severed from my griefs,
And woes by wrong imaginations lose
The knowledge of themselves.
Drum afar off.

EDGAR Give me your hand.
Far off methinks I hear the beaten drum.
Come, father, I'll bestow you with a friend. *Exeunt.*

*

❧ IV.7 *Enter Cordelia, Kent, [Doctor,] and Gentleman.*

CORDELIA
O thou good Kent, how shall I live and work
To match thy goodness? My life will be too short
And every measure fail me.

KENT
To be acknowledged, madam, is o'erpaid.
All my reports go with the modest truth;
Nor more nor clipped, but so.

CORDELIA Be better suited.
These weeds are memories of those worser hours.
I prithee put them off.

KENT Pardon, dear madam.
Yet to be known shortens my made intent.
My boon I make it that you know me not
Till time and I think meet.

CORDELIA
Then be't so, my good lord.
[To the Doctor] How does the king?

---

279 *ingenious* rational, intelligent **280** *distract* mad **282** *wrong imaginations* delusions

IV.7 The French camp **4** *o'erpaid* more than sufficient **5** *go* accord **6** *clipped* less; *suited* dressed **7** *weeds* clothes; *memories* reminders **9** *Yet . . . intent* to reveal myself now would spoil my plan (for Lear to recognize him as Kent) **10** *My . . . it* I ask as my reward **11** *meet* suitable

DOCTOR
Madam, sleeps still.
CORDELIA
O you kind gods,
Cure this great breach in his abusèd nature!
Th' untuned and jarring senses, O, wind up 16
Of this child-changèd father! 17
DOCTOR
So please your majesty
That we may wake the king? He hath slept long.
CORDELIA
Be governed by your knowledge, and proceed 20
I' th' sway of your own will. Is he arrayed? 21
Enter Lear in a chair carried by Servants.
GENTLEMAN
Ay, madam. In the heaviness of sleep
We put fresh garments on him.
DOCTOR
Be by, good madam, when we do awake him.
I doubt not of his temperance. 25
[CORDELIA Very well.
[Music.]
DOCTOR
Please draw near. Louder the music there.]
CORDELIA
O my dear father, restoration hang
Thy medicine on my lips, and let this kiss
Repair those violent harms that my two sisters
Have in thy reverence made. 30
KENT Kind and dear princess.
CORDELIA
Had you not been their father, these white flakes 31

---

16 *jarring* discordant; *wind up* put in tune 17 *child-changèd* (both changed by his children and changed into a child) 21 *I' th' sway . . . will* as you see fit; *arrayed* properly dressed 25 *temperance* self-control 30 *in . . . reverence* on the dignity of your age 31 *flakes* hairs

32 Did challenge pity of them. Was this a face
To be opposed against the jarring winds?
[To stand against the deep dread-bolted thunder?
In the most terrible and nimble stroke
36 Of quick cross lightning to watch, poor perdu,
37 With this thin helm?] Mine enemy's dog,
Though he had bit me, should have stood that night
39 Against my fire; and wast thou fain, poor father,
40 To hovel thee with swine and rogues forlorn
41 In short and musty straw? Alack, alack,
'Tis wonder that thy life and wits at once
Had not concluded all. – He wakes. Speak to him.

DOCTOR
Madam, do you; 'tis fittest.

CORDELIA
How does my royal lord? How fares your majesty?

LEAR
You do me wrong to take me out o' th' grave.
Thou art a soul in bliss; but I am bound
48 Upon a wheel of fire, that mine own tears
Do scald like molten lead.

CORDELIA
Sir, do you know me?

LEAR
50 You are a spirit, I know. Where did you die?

CORDELIA
51 Still, still, far wide!

DOCTOR
He's scarce awake. Let him alone awhile.

LEAR
Where have I been? Where am I? Fair daylight?
54 I am mightily abused. I should e'en die with pity

---

32 *challenge* demand **36** *watch* stand guard; *perdu* an exposed (and expendable) sentry **37** *helm* helmet (i.e., his white hair) **39** *Against* beside; *fain* obliged **41** *short* broken **48** *wheel of fire* (the image combines the wheel on which prisoners were bound for beatings with the burning of heretics or of souls in hell) **51** *wide* wide of the mark **54** *abused* ill-used, deceived

To see another thus. I know not what to say.
I will not swear these are my hands. Let's see –
I feel this pin prick. Would I were assured
Of my condition.

CORDELIA O look upon me, sir,
And hold your hand in benediction o'er me.
You must not kneel.

LEAR 60
Pray, do not mock me.
I am a very foolish fond old man,
Fourscore and upward, not an hour more nor less; 62
And, to deal plainly,
I fear I am not in my perfect mind.
Methinks I should know you, and know this man:
Yet I am doubtful, for I am mainly ignorant 67
What place this is; and all the skill I have
Remembers not these garments; nor I know not
Where I did lodge last night. Do not laugh at me; 70
For, as I am a man, I think this lady
To be my child Cordelia.

CORDELIA And so I am! I am!

LEAR
Be your tears wet? Yes, faith. I pray weep not.
If you have poison for me, I will drink it.
I know you do not love me; for your sisters
Have (as I do remember) done me wrong.
You have some cause, they have not.

CORDELIA No cause, no cause.

LEAR
Am I in France?

KENT In your own kingdom, sir.

LEAR
Do not abuse me. 80

DOCTOR
Be comforted, good madam. The great rage

---

62 *fond* (the word also means foolish) 67 *mainly* entirely 80 *abuse* deceive

You see is killed in him; [and yet it is danger
83 To make him even o'er the time he has lost.]
Desire him to go in. Trouble him no more
85 Till further settling.

CORDELIA
Will't please your highness walk?
You must bear with me.

LEAR
Pray you now, forget and forgive. I am old and foolish.
Exeunt. [Manent Kent and Gentleman.]

[GENTLEMAN Holds it true, sir, that the Duke of Cornwall was so slain?
90 KENT Most certain, sir.
91 GENTLEMAN Who is conductor of his people?
KENT As 'tis said, the bastard son of Gloucester.
GENTLEMAN They say Edgar, his banished son, is with the Earl of Kent in Germany.
95 KENT Report is changeable. 'Tis time to look about; the
96 powers of the kingdom approach apace.
97 GENTLEMAN The arbitrament is like to be bloody. Fare you well, sir. *[Exit.]*

KENT
99 My point and period will be throughly wrought,
100 Or well or ill, as this day's battle's fought. *Exit.*]

*

❧ **V.1** *Enter, with Drum and Colors, Edmund, Regan, Gentleman, and Soldiers.*

EDMUND
1 Know of the duke if his last purpose hold,
2 Or whether since he is advised by aught

---

83 *even o'er* fill in **85** *settling* calm sets in **91** *conductor . . . people* commander of his forces **95** *Report* rumor; *look about* see to our preparations **96** *powers* forces **97** *arbitrament* action **99** *My . . . wrought* my purpose and end will be fully completed **100** *Or* either

V.1 The British camp **1** *Know . . . hold* find out from Albany if his most recent intention (to join in the fight against Cordelia's forces) still holds good **2** *since* since then

To change the course. He's full of alteration
And self-reproving. Bring his constant pleasure. 4
[Exit an Officer.]

REGAN
Our sister's man is certainly miscarried. 5

EDMUND
'Tis to be doubted, madam. 6

REGAN
Now, sweet lord,
You know the goodness I intend upon you.
Tell me, but truly – but then speak the truth –
Do you not love my sister? 9

EDMUND
In honored love.

REGAN
But have you never found my brother's way 10
To the forfended place? 11

[EDMUND That thought abuses you.

REGAN
I am doubtful that you have been conjunct 13
And bosomed with her, as far as we call hers.] 14

EDMUND
No, by mine honor, madam.

REGAN
I never shall endure her. Dear my lord,
Be not familiar with her. 17

EDMUND
Fear me not.
She and the duke her husband!

Enter, with Drum and Colors, Albany, Goneril, Soldiers.

[GONERIL *[Aside]*
I had rather lose the battle than that sister
Should loosen him and me.] 20

---

4 *constant pleasure* firm decision 5 *sister's man* Oswald; *is . . . miscarried* has certainly met with an accident 6 *doubted* feared 9 *honored* honorable 10 *brother's* Albany's 11 *forfended* forbidden; *abuses* is unworthy of 13 *doubtful* suspicious 13–14 *conjunct . . . her* both in complicity with her and her lover 14 *as . . . hers* as completely hers as you can be 17 *familiar* intimate; *fear* doubt

ALBANY
Our very loving sister, well bemet.
Sir, this I heard: the king is come to his daughter,
23 With others whom the rigor of our state
24 Forced to cry out. [Where I could not be honest,
I never yet was valiant. For this business,
26 It touches us as France invades our land,
27 Not bolds the king with others, whom I fear
28 Most just and heavy causes make oppose.
EDMUND
29 Sir, you speak nobly.]
REGAN Why is this reasoned?
GONERIL
30 Combine together 'gainst the enemy;
31 For these domestic and particular broils
32 Are not the question here.
ALBANY Let's then determine
33 With th' ancient of war on our proceeding.
[EDMUND
I shall attend you presently at your tent.]
REGAN
Sister, you'll go with us?
GONERIL No.
REGAN
37 'Tis most convenient. Pray go with us.
GONERIL
38 O ho, I know the riddle. – I will go.
Exeunt both the Armies.

Enter Edgar.

---

23 *rigor . . . state* harshness of our rule 24 *be honest* behave honorably 26 *touches* concerns 27 *Not bolds* not because he emboldens 28 *heavy* serious 29 *Why . . . reasoned* i.e., why are you telling us this 30 *Combine together* let us join our forces 31 *particular broils* private quarrels 32 *question* issue 33 *th' ancient of war* experienced senior officers 37 *convenient* proper that you do 38 *I . . . riddle* I get the point (which is to prevent her from being alone with Edmund)

EDGAR *[To Albany]*
If e'er your grace had speech with man so poor,
Hear me one word. *40*
ALBANY *[To those departing]*
I'll overtake you. *[To Edgar]* Speak.
EDGAR
Before you fight the battle, ope this letter.
If you have victory, let the trumpet sound
For him that brought it. Wretched though I seem,
I can produce a champion that will prove 44
What is avouchèd there. If you miscarry, 45
Your business of the world hath so an end,
And machination ceases. Fortune love you. 47
ALBANY
Stay till I have read the letter.
EDGAR I was forbid it.
When time shall serve, let but the herald cry,
And I'll appear again. *50*
ALBANY
Why, fare thee well. I will o'erlook thy paper. 51
Exit [Edgar].

Enter Edmund.

EDMUND
The enemy's in view; draw up your powers.
Here is the guess of their true strength and forces 53
By diligent discovery; but your haste 54
Is now urged on you. 55
ALBANY We will greet the time. *Exit.*
EDMUND
To both these sisters have I sworn my love;
Each jealous of the other, as the stung 57

---

44 *prove* establish as true (in a trial by single combat) **45** *avouchèd* asserted; *miscarry* lose the battle **47** *machination* plotting **51 s.d.** (Presumably Albany has no time to read Oswald's letter before Edmund's entrance) **53** *guess* estimate **54** *discovery* spying **55** *greet the time* be ready when the time comes **57** *jealous* suspicious; *stung* those who have been bitten

Are of the adder. Which of them shall I take?
Both? One? Or neither? Neither can be enjoyed,
60 If both remain alive. To take the widow
Exasperates, makes mad her sister Goneril;
62 And hardly shall I carry out my side,
Her husband being alive. Now then, we'll use
64 His countenance for the battle, which being done,
Let her who would be rid of him devise
66 His speedy taking off. As for the mercy
Which he intends to Lear and to Cordelia –
The battle done, and they within our power,
69 Shall never see his pardon; for my state
70 Stands on me to defend, not to debate. *Exit.*

*

❧ V.2 *Alarum within. Enter, with Drum and Colors, Lear, [held by the hand by] Cordelia; and Soldiers [of France], over the stage and exeunt.*
Enter Edgar and Gloucester.

EDGAR
1 Here, father, take the shadow of this tree
2 For your good host. Pray that the right may thrive.
If ever I return to you again,
4 I'll bring you comfort.
GLOUCESTER Grace go with you, sir.
Exit [Edgar].

Alarum and retreat within. Enter Edgar.

EDGAR
Away, old man! Give me thy hand. Away!
King Lear hath lost, he and his daughter ta'en.

---

62 *carry . . . side* accomplish my plan 64 *countenance* authority, backing 66 *taking off* murder 69 *Shall* they shall 69–70 *state . . . me* situation requires me

V.2 A field **s.d.** *Alarum within* trumpets offstage 1 *father* old man (Edgar still has not revealed his identity to Gloucester) 2 *host* shelter **4 s.d.** *retreat* i.e., sound of retreating army

Give me thy hand. Come on.

GLOUCESTER

No further, sir. A man may rot even here.

EDGAR

What, in ill thoughts again? Men must endure
Their going hence, even as their coming hither; 10
Ripeness is all. Come on. 11

GLOUCESTER And that's true too. *Exeunt.*

*

☙ V.3 *Enter, in conquest, with Drum and Colors, Edmund; Lear and Cordelia as prisoners; Soldiers, Captain.*

EDMUND

Some officers take them away. Good guard
Until their greater pleasures first be known 2
That are to censure them. 3

CORDELIA We are not the first
Who with best meaning have incurred the worst. 4
For thee, oppressèd king, I am cast down;
Myself could else outfrown false Fortune's frown. 6
Shall we not see these daughters and these sisters?

LEAR

No, no, no, no! Come, let's away to prison.
We two alone will sing like birds i' th' cage.
When thou dost ask me blessing, I'll kneel down 10
And ask of thee forgiveness. So we'll live,
And pray, and sing, and tell old tales, and laugh
At gilded butterflies, and hear poor rogues
Talk of court news; and we'll talk with them too –
Who loses and who wins; who's in, who's out –
And take upon's the mystery of things

---

11 *Ripeness is all* i.e., the gods decree when fruit is ripe and falls; coming to that ripeness is all that matters

V.3 The British camp 2 *their . . . pleasures* the wishes of those in command 3 *censure* pass judgment on 4 *meaning* intentions 6 *else* otherwise

As if we were God's spies; and we'll wear out,
In a walled prison, packs and sects of great ones
That ebb and flow by th' moon.

EDMUND Take them away.

LEAR
Upon such sacrifices, my Cordelia,
The gods themselves throw incense. Have I caught thee?
He that parts us shall bring a brand from heaven
And fire us hence like foxes. Wipe thine eyes.
The good years shall devour them, flesh and fell,
Ere they shall make us weep! We'll see 'em starved first.
Come. *Exeunt [Lear and Cordelia, guarded].*

EDMUND
Come hither, captain; hark.
Take thou this note.
[Gives a paper.] Go follow them to prison.
One step I have advanced thee. If thou dost
As this instructs thee, thou dost make thy way
To noble fortunes. Know thou this, that men
Are as the time is. To be tender-minded
Does not become a sword. Thy great employment
Will not bear question. Either say thou'lt do't,
Or thrive by other means.

CAPTAIN I'll do't, my lord.

EDMUND
About it; and write happy when thou'st done.
Mark, I say instantly, and carry it so
As I have set it down.

---

17 *wear out* outlast **18** *packs and sects* parties and factions **19** *That . . . moon* whose power changes monthly **21** *throw incense* are celebrants; *Have . . . thee* i.e., do I really have you again **22** *brand* torch; i.e., it will take divine powers to separate us now **24** *good years* passage of time, old age; *flesh . . . fell* meat and skin, entirely **28** *advanced* promoted **31** *Are . . . is* i.e., must seize their opportunities **32** *sword* i.e., soldier **33** *question* discussion **35** *write happy* call yourself fortunate **36** *carry it* carry it out

[CAPTAIN
I cannot draw a cart, nor eat dried oats –
If it be a man's work, I'll do't.] *Exit.*

Flourish. Enter Albany, Goneril, Regan, Soldiers.

ALBANY
Sir, you have showed today your valiant strain,
And fortune led you well. You have the captives
Who were the opposites of this day's strife.
I do require them of you, so to use them
As we shall find their merits and our safety
May equally determine.

EDMUND
Sir, I thought it fit
To send the old and miserable king
To some retention [and appointed guard];
Whose age had charms in it, whose title more,
To pluck the common bosom on his side
And turn our impressed lances in our eyes
Which do command them. With him I sent the queen,
My reason all the same; and they are ready
Tomorrow, or at further space, t' appear
Where you shall hold your session. [At this time
We sweat and bleed, the friend hath lost his friend,
And the best quarrels, in the heat, are cursed
By those that feel their sharpness.
The question of Cordelia and her father
Requires a fitter place.]

ALBANY Sir, by your patience,
I hold you but a subject of this war,
Not as a brother.

---

38 *draw . . . oats* i.e., I'm a man, not a horse **40** *strain* both qualities and lineage **42** *opposites of* opponents in **43** *use* treat **48** *retention* detention **50** *pluck . . . on* draw popular sympathy to **51** *turn . . . eyes* i.e., turn our soldiers against us; *impressed lances* drafted pikemen **54** *further space* a later time **55** *session* court hearing **57** *best . . . heat* most just wars in the heat of battle **58** *feel . . . sharpness* endure their pain **61** *subject of* subordinate in

REGAN That's as we list to grace him.
Methinks our pleasure might have been demanded
Ere you had spoke so far. He led our powers,
Bore the commission of my place and person,
The which immediacy may well stand up
And call itself your brother.
GONERIL Not so hot!
In his own grace he doth exalt himself
More than in your addition.
REGAN In my rights
By me invested, he compeers the best.
ALBANY
That were the most if he should husband you.
REGAN
Jesters do oft prove prophets.
GONERIL Holla, holla!
That eye that told you so looked but asquint.
REGAN
Lady, I am not well; else I should answer
From a full-flowing stomach. General,
Take thou my soldiers, prisoners, patrimony;
Dispose of them, of me; the walls is thine.
Witness the world that I create thee here
My lord and master.
GONERIL Mean you to enjoy him?
ALBANY
The let-alone lies not in your good will.
EDMUND
Nor in thine, lord.

---

62 *we list* I please **63** *pleasure . . . demanded* wishes should have been consulted **65** *Bore . . . person* i.e., acted with my authority **66** *immediacy* present status (as my deputy) **67** *hot* fast **68** *grace* merit **69** *your addition* the honors conferred by you **70** *compeers* equals **71** *the most* i.e., the most complete investiture with your rights **73** *asquint* cross-eyed, i.e., jealously **75** *stomach* anger **76** *patrimony* inheritance **77** *the . . . thine* i.e., you have captured my castle **80** *let-alone* both permission and veto

ALBANY Half-blooded fellow, yes.
REGAN *[To Edmund]*
Let the drum strike, and prove my title thine. 82
ALBANY
Stay yet; hear reason. Edmund, I arrest thee
On capital treason; and, in thy attaint, 84
[Points to Goneril.] This gilded serpent.
[To Regan] For your claim, fair sister,
I bar it in the interest of my wife.
'Tis she is subcontracted to this lord, 87
And I, her husband, contradict your banns. 88
If you will marry, make your loves to me; 89
My lady is bespoke. 90
GONERIL An interlude!
ALBANY
Thou art armed, Gloucester. Let the trumpet sound.
If none appear to prove upon thy person
Thy heinous, manifest, and many treasons,
There is my pledge. 94
[Throws down a glove.] I'll make it on thy heart,
Ere I taste bread, thou art in nothing less 95
Than I have here proclaimed thee.
REGAN Sick, O sick!
GONERIL *[Aside]*
If not, I'll ne'er trust medicine. 97
EDMUND
There's my exchange. 98
[Throws down a glove.] What in the world he is
That names me traitor, villainlike he lies.
Call by the trumpet. He that dares approach, *100*

---

81 *Half-blooded* illegitimate (and only half noble) **82** *drum strike* as a signal to prepare for battle **84** *in . . . attaint* in complicity with your crimes **87** *subcontracted* (because she is already contracted, by marriage, to Albany) **88** *banns* declaration of an intention to marry **89** *make . . . to* woo **90** *bespoke* already spoken for; *interlude* farce **94** *make* prove **95** *nothing less* no way less guilty **97** *medicine* i.e., poison **98** *What . . . world* whoever

On him, on you, who not? I will maintain
My truth and honor firmly.

ALBANY
A herald, ho!

[EDMUND A herald, ho, a herald!]

ALBANY
104 Trust to thy single virtue; for thy soldiers,
All levied in my name, have in my name
Took their discharge.

REGAN My sickness grows upon me.

ALBANY
She is not well. Convey her to my tent.
[Exit Regan, attended.]

Enter a Herald.

Come hither, herald. Let the trumpet sound,
And read out this.

110 [CAPTAIN Sound, trumpet!]

A trumpet sounds.

HERALD *[Reads.]* "If any man of quality or degree within the lists of the army will maintain upon Edmund, supposed Earl of Gloucester, that he is a manifold traitor, let him appear by the third sound of the trumpet. He is bold in his defense."

[EDMUND Sound!]

First trumpet.

HERALD Again!

Second trumpet.

118 Again!

Third trumpet.

Trumpet answers within.

Enter Edgar, armed [at the third sound, a Trumpeter before him].

---

104 *single virtue* unaided strength **118 s.d.** *armed* (Edgar wears a helmet with the beaver down, covering his face)

ALBANY
Ask him his purposes, why he appears
Upon this call o' th' trumpet. *120*
HERALD What are you?
Your name, your quality, and why you answer 121
This present summons?
EDGAR Know my name is lost,
By treason's tooth bare-gnawn and canker-bit; 123
Yet am I noble as the adversary
I come to cope. 125
ALBANY Which is that adversary?
EDGAR
What's he that speaks for Edmund Earl of Gloucester?
EDMUND
Himself. What sayst thou to him?
EDGAR Draw thy sword.
That, if my speech offend a noble heart,
Thy arm may do thee justice. Here is mine.
[Draws his sword.]
Behold it is my privilege, *130*
The privilege of mine honors,
My oath, and my profession. I protest – 132
Maugre thy strength, place, youth, and eminence, 133
Despite thy victor sword and fire-new fortune, 134
Thy valor and thy heart – thou art a traitor, 135
False to thy gods, thy brother, and thy father,
Conspirant 'gainst this high illustrious prince, 137
And from th' extremest upward of thy head 138
To the descent and dust below thy foot 139
A most toad-spotted traitor. Say thou "no," 140
This sword, this arm, and my best spirits are bent

---

121 *quality* rank 123 *treason's* treachery's; *canker-bit* eaten away by worms 125 *cope* encounter 132 *profession* i.e., as a knight 133 *Maugre* despite 134 *fire-new* newly forged 135 *heart* courage 137 *Conspirant* conspirator 138 *upward* top 139 *descent* lowest part 140 *toad-spotted* venomous, reptilian

To prove upon thy heart, whereto I speak,
143 Thou liest.

EDMUND In wisdom I should ask thy name,
But since thy outside looks so fair and warlike,
145 And that thy tongue some say of breeding breathes,
146 What safe and nicely I might well delay
147 By rule of knighthood I disdain and spurn.
Back do I toss these treasons to thy head,
149 With the hell-hated lie o'erwhelm thy heart,
150 Which – for they yet glance by and scarcely bruise –
151 This sword of mine shall give them instant way
Where they shall rest forever. Trumpets, speak!
Alarums. Fight. [Edmund falls.]

ALBANY
153 Save him, save him.

GONERIL This is practice, Gloucester.
By th' law of war thou wast not bound to answer
155 An unknown opposite. Thou art not vanquished,
156 But cozened and beguiled.

ALBANY Shut your mouth, dame,
Or with this paper shall I stop it. – Hold, sir. –
[To Goneril]
Thou worse than any name, read thine own evil.
No tearing, lady! I perceive you know it.

GONERIL
160 Say if I do – the laws are mine, not thine.
161 Who can arraign me for't?

ALBANY Most monstrous! O,
Know'st thou this paper?

---

143 *In . . . name* (because one was not obliged to fight with an inferior, nor with an unknown adversary) **145** *say* touch, sign **146** *safe and nicely* cautiously and correctly **147** *disdain and spurn* i.e., to ask what I am entitled to know **149** *hell-hated* hateful as hell **150** *Which – for they* since those treasons **151** *way* access **153** *Save him* i.e., don't kill him; *This is practice* i.e., you've been tricked **155** *opposite* opponent **156** *cozened* cheated **160** *the . . . mine* (Goneril is queen; Albany is her consort) **161** *arraign* try; the monarch, having no peers, could not be prosecuted

GONERIL Ask me not what I know.
Exit.

ALBANY
Go after her. She's desperate; govern her. 163
[Exit an Officer.]

EDMUND
What you have charged me with, that have I done,
And more, much more. The time will bring it out.
'Tis past, and so am I. – But what art thou
That hast this fortune on me? If thou'rt noble, 167
I do forgive thee. 168

EDGAR Let's exchange charity.
I am no less in blood than thou art, Edmund;
If more, the more thou'st wronged me. *170*
My name is Edgar and thy father's son.
The gods are just, and of our pleasant vices 172
Make instruments to plague us.
The dark and vicious place where thee he got 174
Cost him his eyes.

EDMUND Thou'st spoken right; 'tis true.
The wheel is come full circle; I am here. 176

ALBANY
Methought thy very gait did prophesy
A royal nobleness. I must embrace thee.
Let sorrow split my heart if ever I
Did hate thee, or thy father. *180*

EDGAR Worthy prince, I know't.

ALBANY
Where have you hid yourself?
How have you known the miseries of your father?

EDGAR
By nursing them, my lord. List a brief tale; 184

---

163 *govern* take care of **167** *fortune on* victory over **168** *charity* forgiveness **172** *pleasant* pleasurable **174** *dark . . . place* adulterous bed, illicit genitals; *got* begot **176** *I . . . here* i.e., at the bottom of Fortune's wheel again **184** *List* hear

And when 'tis told, O that my heart would burst!
186 The bloody proclamation to escape
187 That followed me so near (O our lives' sweetness,
That we the pain of death would hourly die
Rather than die at once!) taught me to shift
190 Into a madman's rags, t' assume a semblance
That very dogs disdained; and in this habit
192 Met I my father with his bleeding rings,
Their precious stones new lost; became his guide,
Led him, begged for him, saved him from despair;
Never – O fault! – revealed myself unto him
Until some half hour past, when I was armed,
Not sure, though hoping of this good success,
I asked his blessing, and from first to last
Told him our pilgrimage. But his flawed heart –
200 Alack, too weak the conflict to support –
'Twixt two extremes of passion, joy and grief,
Burst smilingly.

EDMUND This speech of yours hath moved me,
And shall perchance do good; but speak you on –
You look as you had something more to say.

ALBANY
If there be more, more woeful, hold it in,
206 For I am almost ready to dissolve,
207 Hearing of this.

[EDGAR This would have seemed a period
208 To such as love not sorrow; but another,
To amplify too much, would make much more,
210 And top extremity.
211 Whilst I was big in clamor, came there in a man,
212 Who, having seen me in my worst estate,
Shunned my abhorred society; but then, finding

---

186 *bloody proclamation* (declaring him an outlaw) **187** *our . . . sweetness* how sweet life is to us **192** *rings* sockets **206** *dissolve* (in tears) **207** *a period* the limit **208–10** *another . . . extremity* to describe another sorrow too fully would exceed the limit **211** *big in clamor* loudly lamenting **212** *in . . . estate* at my worst

Who 'twas that so endured, with his strong arms
He fastened on my neck, and bellowed out
As he'd burst heaven, threw him on my father, 216
Told the most piteous tale of Lear and him
That ever ear received; which in recounting
His grief grew puissant, and the strings of life 219
Began to crack. Twice then the trumpets sounded, *220*
And there I left him tranced.

ALBANY But who was this?

EDGAR
Kent, sir, the banished Kent; who in disguise
Followed his enemy king and did him service
Improper for a slave.]

Enter a Gentleman [with a bloody knife].

GENTLEMAN
Help, help! O, help!

EDGAR What kind of help?

ALBANY Speak, man.

EDGAR
What means this bloody knife?

GENTLEMAN 'Tis hot, it smokes.
It came even from the heart of – O, she's dead.

ALBANY
Who dead? Speak, man. *230*

GENTLEMAN
Your lady, sir, your lady; and her sister
By her is poisonèd; she confesses it.

EDMUND
I was contracted to them both. All three
Now marry in an instant. 234

EDGAR Here comes Kent.

Enter Kent.

ALBANY
Produce the bodies, be they alive or dead.
[Exit Gentleman.]

---

216 *As* as if; *him* himself 219 *puissant* powerful 234 *marry* unite

This judgment of the heavens, that makes us tremble,
Touches us not with pity. – O, is this he?
The time will not allow the compliment
Which very manners urges.

KENT I am come
240 To bid my king and master aye good night.
Is he not here?

ALBANY Great thing of us forgot!
Speak, Edmund, where's the king? and where's Cordelia?
Goneril and Regan's bodies brought out.
243 Seest thou this object, Kent?

KENT
Alack, why thus?

EDMUND Yet Edmund was beloved.
The one the other poisoned for my sake,
And after slew herself.

ALBANY
Even so. Cover their faces.

EDMUND
I pant for life. Some good I mean to do,
Despite of mine own nature. Quickly send –
250 Be brief in it – to th' castle, for my writ
Is on the life of Lear and on Cordelia.
Nay, send in time.

ALBANY Run, run, O run!

EDGAR
254 To who, my lord? Who has the office? Send
Thy token of reprieve.

EDMUND
Well thought on. Take my sword;
Give it the captain.

EDGAR Haste thee for thy life. *[Exit Officer.]*

EDMUND
He hath commission from thy wife and me

---

240 *aye* forever 243 *object* sight, spectacle 250 *brief* quick; *writ* order of execution 254 *office* commission

To hang Cordelia in the prison and
To lay the blame upon her own despair 260
That she fordid herself. 261

ALBANY
The gods defend her! Bear him hence awhile.
[Edmund is borne off.]

Enter Lear, with Cordelia in his arms [, Gentleman, and others following].

LEAR
Howl, howl, howl! O, you are men of stones.
Had I your tongues and eyes, I'd use them so
That heaven's vault should crack. She's gone forever.
I know when one is dead, and when one lives.
She's dead as earth. Lend me a looking glass.
If that her breath will mist or stain the stone, 268
Why then she lives. 269

KENT Is this the promised end?

EDGAR
Or image of that horror? 270

ALBANY Fall and cease.

LEAR
This feather stirs; she lives! If it be so,
It is a chance which does redeem all sorrows
That ever I have felt.

KENT O my good master.

LEAR
Prithee away.

EDGAR 'Tis noble Kent, your friend.

LEAR
A plague upon you murderers, traitors all;
I might have saved her; now she's gone forever.
Cordelia, Cordelia, stay a little. Ha,
What is't thou sayst? Her voice was ever soft,

---

261 *fordid* destroyed **268** *stone* mirror of polished stone **269** *promised end* Judgment Day **270** *Fall . . . cease* let the world end

Gentle, and low – an excellent thing in woman.
280 I killed the slave that was a-hanging thee.

GENTLEMAN

'Tis true, my lords, he did.

LEAR Did I not, fellow?

282 I have seen the day, with my good biting falchion
I would have made them skip. I am old now,
284 And these same crosses spoil me. Who are you?
Mine eyes are not o' th' best, I'll tell you straight.

KENT

286 If Fortune brag of two she loved and hated,
One of them we behold.

LEAR

288 This is a dull sight. Are you not Kent?

KENT

289 Your servant Kent; where is your servant Caius?

LEAR

290 He's a good fellow, I can tell you that.
He'll strike, and quickly too. He's dead and rotten.

KENT

No, my good lord; I am the very man.

LEAR

293 I'll see that straight.

KENT

294 That from your first of difference and decay
295 Have followed your sad steps.

LEAR You are welcome hither.

KENT

296 Nor no man else. All's cheerless, dark, and deadly.

---

282 *falchion* small sword **284** *crosses spoil* vexations weaken **286** *loved and hated* first loved, then hated (Lear and a hypothetical other? Lear and Cordelia? Lear and Kent, who are looking at each other?) **288** *dull sight* dismal spectacle **289** *Caius* (obviously Kent's alias; but the name appears nowhere else in the play) **293** *I'll . . . straight* I'll attend to it shortly **294** *difference and decay* quarrel and decline **295** *You . . . hither* (Lear fails to make the connection) **296** *Nor . . . else* i.e., no one is welcome here

Your eldest daughters have fordone themselves, 297
And desperately are dead. 298

LEAR Ay, so I think.

ALBANY
He knows not what he says; and vain is it
That we present us to him. 300

EDGAR Very bootless.

Enter a Messenger.

MESSENGER
Edmund is dead, my lord.

ALBANY That's but a trifle here.
You lords and noble friends, know our intent.
What comfort to this great decay may come 304
Shall be applied. For us, we will resign,
During the life of this old majesty,
To him our absolute power; *[To Edgar and Kent]* you to your rights,
With boot and such addition as your honors 308
Have more than merited. All friends shall taste
The wages of their virtue, and all foes *310*
The cup of their deservings. – O, see, see!

LEAR
And my poor fool is hanged: no, no, no life? 312
Why should a dog, a horse, a rat, have life,
And thou no breath at all? Thou'lt come no more,
Never, never, never, never, never.
Pray you undo this button. Thank you, sir.
Do you see this? Look on her! Look, her lips,
Look there, look there –

He dies.

EDGAR He faints. My lord, my lord –

---

297 *fordone* killed **298** *desperately* in despair **300** *bootless* pointless **304** *decay* ruin, Lear **308** *boot* reward; *addition* advancement in rank **312** *fool* (A term of endearment; here, Cordelia. The fool disappears after III.6.)

KENT
Break, heart, I prithee break!
EDGAR Look up, my lord.
KENT
320 Vex not his ghost. O, let him pass! He hates him
321 That would upon the rack of this tough world
Stretch him out longer.
EDGAR He is gone indeed.
KENT
The wonder is he hath endured so long;
He but usurped his life.
ALBANY
Bear them from hence. Our present business
Is general woe.
[To Kent and Edgar] Friends of my soul, you twain
327 Rule in this realm, and the gored state sustain.
KENT
I have a journey, sir, shortly to go.
My master calls me; I must not say no.
EDGAR
330 The weight of this sad time we must obey,
Speak what we feel, not what we ought to say.
The oldest hath borne most; we that are young
Shall never see so much, nor live so long.
Exeunt with a dead march.

---

320 *ghost* spirit 321 *rack* a torture instrument 327 *gored* wounded

AVAILABLE FROM PENGUIN BOOKS

King Lear

Edited by Stephen Orgel

Hamlet

Edited by A. R. Braunmuller

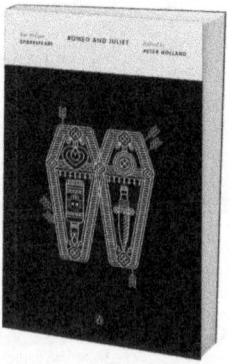

Romeo and Juliet

Edited by Peter Holland

Macbeth

Edited by Stephen Orgel

PENGUIN
BOOKS

AVAILABLE FROM PENGUIN CLASSICS

The Complete Pelican Shakespeare

Since *The Complete Pelican Shakespeare* debuted more than forty years ago, developments in scholarship have revolutionized our understanding of William Shakespeare. The general editors of the series and world-renowned Shakespeareans, Stephen Orgel of Stanford University, and A. R. Braunmuller of UCLA, dedicated seven years to incorporating the most up-to-date research and debate about the Bard, making this revised edition the premier choice for students, teachers, academics, and general readers for decades to come.

PENGUIN BOOKS